ENCHANTED EMPORIUM

4

Enchanted Emporium is published by Stone Arch Books
A Capstone imprint
1710 Roe Crest Drive
North Mankato, Minnesota 56003
www.capstonepub.com

First published in the United States in 2015 by Capstone

© 2013 Atlantyca Dreamfarm s.r.l., Italy
© 2016 for this book in English language (Capstone Young Readers)
Text by Pierdomenico Baccalario
Illustrations by Iacopo Bruno
Translated by Nanette McGuinness
Original edition published by Edizioni Piemme S.p.A., Italy
Original title: La ladra di specchi

Cataloging-in-Publication Data is available on the Library of Congress website.
ISBN: 978-1-4965-0516-3 (library binding)
ISBN: 978-1-4965-0517-0 (paperback)
ISBN: 978-1-62370-259-5 (paper-over-board)
ISBN: 978-1-4965-2314-3 (eBook)

Summary: Aiby Lily is in danger! A special reunion of the Enchanted Emporium's shopkeeper families turned out to be a deadly trap — and Lily's talented father is powerless to stop it. Now Finley McPhee needs to rescue his friend and find out where the meeting of the seven families is being held, all while fending off the evil Semueld Askell. But along the way, Finley will finally come face to face with a part of himself that he never wanted to meet.

Designer: Alison Thiele

Printed in China.
03312015   008866RRDF15

THE THIEF OF MIRRORS

by Pierdomenico Baccalario · Illustrations by Iacopo Bruno

STONE ARCH BOOKS

a capstone imprint

TABLE OF CONTENTS

ANTS,
LEADERS, &
COFFEE GROUNDS

The ants crept across the walls. They moved in single-file lines parallel to each other. It was like they knew exactly where they wanted to go, and why.

That's why I admired them. Well, I admired them for more reasons than that, but I have never been someone who understands things clearly. More often than not, I know them intuitively. Unfortunately, most people don't put much stock in my gut feelings. Maybe that's the reason I'll have to repeat my previous school year. To be fair, the seventy-one days I spent fishing at the stream instead of attending class might have contributed to that outcome. But I never liked books very much — that is, until the Lilys arrived in town. But then gain, things were never easy for me.

There are many things we all believe to be true that actually aren't. Even things written in books. But now isn't the right time to talk about them.

About books, I mean. And soon you'll see why.

I was having one of the best summers of my life. Or at least it *had* been until my brother, Doug, ruined everything.

In Applecross, the town in northern Scotland where I lived, no one could remember such weather. We had eight consecutive days of sun without the slightest drizzle. Even the mosquitoes seemed stunned, arriving at nightfall and buzzing softly only at sea level. The ants, however, seemed completely indifferent to the weird weather. Their job was to stock up for winter, and they shuffled in single file along the cracks in the floor. They seemed to know where they were going, but how?

I still hadn't figured it out, but I was conducting a scientific experiment. I'd already tried crushing the first ant in the line twice. I figured that eliminating the leader of their mysterious campaign would throw them into chaos. But after a moment of understandable confusion, the unfortunate leader's second-in-command stepped up and took its place at the front of the line. And the others marched onward as if nothing had happened.

"See, Patches?" I told my trusty dog. "They can all be leaders. And when one leads, the rest follow."

He wagged his tail and tried to lick my face with his usual enthusiasm. He was a strong, stubborn mutt with furry ears and a rocket-shaped tail. He belonged to a mongrel breed that nonetheless kept the same distinct features across generations. Patches was actually the fourth dog named Patches to live at the McPhee home.

Speaking of which, perhaps I should mention that the person writing the story of that summer — which now seems so long ago — is still me, Finley McPhee. And yes, it's still Finley with an "F."

Anyway, I was furious that evening. You may think it's creepy to stay shut up in your room killing ants, but I had a good reason for doing so: better the ants than my brother.

My mom must have entered my room quietly, or maybe I'd been concentrating so hard that I didn't hear her come in. When she spoke, I was so startled that I scampered back against the wall and almost swallowed my tongue.

"Good heavens!" Mom exclaimed, recoiling. The two of us broke into laughter. "I just came in to ask you what you want for dinner," she added.

"I've got ants in my room," I said, figuring I should explain why I was lying on the ground.

"It's a sign," she said. I squinted at her. "Ants go where there's something to eat. I'd say there's some leftover food under your bed."

Under my bed was the box with the false bottom, where I kept my most precious things that I didn't want my brother to see. It contained two messages I had found in bottles that came from the sea, a Borderpassing coin I'd found in my pocket, two weird pieces of iron, and five or six oddly shaped rocks. They were all cataloged with their own detailed labels. In short: nothing ants would want to eat.

My mom knelt down next to me and patted my hand. Patches wagged his tail in front of her face and circled a few times before climbing into her lap.

Mom pointed at the column of ants on the wood floor. "If you don't want them to go under your bed, you should get some coffee," she said.

"Why will the ants go away if I get some coffee?" I asked.

My mom smiled. "You have to build a barrier of mint, cinnamon, or coffee grounds on the floor," she explained. "And to be extra safe, you should make a second one with lemon juice."

I looked at her, considering it. "Really?"

She nodded. "Really. They don't like strong odors."

We sat there a little longer, watching them without speaking. It was a nice moment — one of those times when you want to say lots of things but don't for fear of ruining it.

"Is everything okay, Finley?" she asked me. "It seems like you're in a morose mood."

"Everything's fine," I said

Well, lots of things were fine. But not all of them.

Chapter
TWO

A STANDOFF,
LOST PUDDING, &
A PUDDLE

"Hi, there, Viper," my big brother greeted me upon his return.

I thought Doug looked like an overgrown doll, but I didn't say anything. He pulled his boots out of the mosquito netting and entered barefoot. He peeked into the kitchen to see what mom was cooking.

"Do I have time to take a shower?" he asked, chipper as a squirrel.

I kept staring at him while he whistled and generally acted as if nothing had happened. He climbed up the stairs and stopped when I blocked his path.

"What's that in your hands?" he asked me, continuing his infuriating nice-guy act. I had a fistful of mint leaves,

cinnamon, and coffee beans in my hands. I barely stopped myself from rubbing them in his face.

"We have to talk," I hissed.

Doug snorted. "Go ahead. I'm listening, Viper."

"Don't call me that," I said.

Doug shrugged his shoulders. "As you wish. Sorry about this whole business. I know you're still upset."

"I'm not upset," I said. "I'm furious. And I want my key back."

"It's my key now," Doug said.

"Only because I gave it to you," I said.

"If it was so important, you should have held onto it," Doug said.

"We had an agreement, Doug!" I snarled. "I only lent it to you. And you kept it!"

His face took on the expression of a deer in headlights. Then he crossed his arms. How could I get that colossal empty head of his to understand?

Doug tried to move around, but I stayed in his face.

"Oh, cut it out," he said. "If you want that key, you can take it back whenever you wish."

"No, I can't!" I said.

And that right there was the whole point. If Doug didn't give me back the key voluntarily, it would return to him even if I stole it back. It was a magical object, with its own rules and stipulations — just like everything else that was sold or repaired at the Enchanted Emporium.

Doug's empty smile seemed downright evil. I would have punched him right then and there, but Mom checked in on us.

"Everything okay, boys?" Mom intervened from downstairs.

"Sure, everything's fine!" Doug answered for both of us. He stuck his hands under my armpits and easily lifted me off the ground. "There's just this insect on the stairs," he added, staring me right in the eyes.

He deflected my kick and tossed me onto the stairs. Relying on my agility, I landed mostly gracefully in a crouched position. I petted Patches and sighed. "Good guys always lose because they refuse to break the rules," I told him.

* * *

At dinner, my father was in an exceptionally good mood. Apparently things had improved at the farm after a period when the sheep had been making life difficult for him. He told us about a livestock show he wanted to participate in, and asked Doug and me if we wanted to go with him. (I replied with a grunt.) He added that there was also a dog breeding competition. My mom laughed, joking that we should sign up Patches.

I didn't find anything funny. All the laughter just managed to irritate me even more. No one in the house seemed to realize how much I was suffering.

But in reality, I think they were forcing themselves to be more cheerful than usual in the hopes that it'd make me feel better. It was well intentioned but completely useless. I asked to be excused before dinner was over.

I walked out the front door and jumped on my bicycle with the invisible seat. As a surprise, my mom had made tapioca pudding with blueberries for dessert, which is my favorite. Assuming I'd already left, she spoke to my dad in a way that sounded worried and sad. "He's not going to the Lily's house again, is he?" she asked. I leaned against the wall next to the kitchen window to listen.

"I don't know," Dad said, shaking his head. "I'll talk to Reverend Prospero tomorrow," he added, as if that was the obvious solution to all my problems.

They kept talking. My mom said she was convinced I was angry because of the family that had recently come to town, the Lilys. Locan, an odd shopkeeper of ancient items, and Aiby, his young daughter. Together they ran the strange, red-walled Enchanted Emporium. My father, however, had gotten it into his head that my discontent was due to the jobs the reverend of Applecross was assigning me that summer.

They were both wrong.

"I'll go speak to him myself," Doug said before our parents could ask him if he knew anything. Then he ate his dessert as well as mine.

I pedaled like mad to get to my beach. Not that it was really mine, but I felt like it was. It was a cove just below a bend in the coastal road. You could see all the houses of Applecross lined up in rows from there. It was a steep pebble beach where sea currents often brought in long bundles of dark algae. And it was secluded due to the swarms of mosquitoes that made it unappealing to tourists and summer campers.

That beach was where I had found my first message in a bottle. And from that beach, in the purple evening light, you could see the little reef with the wooden tower where I kissed Aiby the first time.

And maybe the last time, too.

I left my bicycle on the side of the road and raced up to the highest point along the cliff. The wind seized me with its mysterious force. My shirt flapped at my ribs. I spread my arms and vented all the rage I'd been nursing in one furious roar.

I screamed at the wind, the sea and the islands that rose from it, the cliff, the pebbles, the mosquitoes, even the seaweed. My long, horrible howl left Patches mute.

I felt much better: exhausted and trembling, but relieved.

I let the wind move me down to the water's edge. I searched for a flat stone and threw it across the waves, skipping it in the direction of the several islands that dotted the bay.

I felt betrayed. By Doug, and by Aiby, too. The key we were fighting over was my key to the shop, the Enchanted Emporium. There were four keys in all: one for the shopkeeper, one for the seeker, one for the repairperson, and one for the defender.

I had parted with the defender key in order to set a trap for Semueld Askell, the man who had wanted to destroy the Enchanted Emporium. The trap worked: Askell was dead. Well, not exactly dead. He'd been turned into a pillar of salt. Either way, I'd risked everything and I'd succeeded.

Except for one tiny little detail: Doug didn't want to give the key back to me because he liked Aiby and wanted an excuse to be around her more.

And Aiby, well . . .

Patches barked. I turned around to see Doug standing on the slope, silhouetted against the sky. He leaned over my bike and pretended to inspect it. Then he shoved his hands into his pockets and walked over to me.

Without speaking, he reached down and grabbed a few pebbles. He rolled them between his fingers, then handed me a flat white one. It was the kind of stone he had a knack for finding — the perfect one for skipping across the waves.

"Listen, Viper," he began. "I'm sorry for all that's happened between us."

"You know perfectly well how to fix it," I said.

"You're right," he admitted. He thrust a hand into his pocket and pulled out a wooden puppet wrapped in a sheet of tissue paper. A note was written on it: *Angelica, for Finley.*

"Aiby told me to give you this," he said. "It's been two days since you've seen them."

"Why do you care?" I said.

Splish-splash.

Doug rested the puppet against a rock. *Why would Aiby want me to have a doll?* I wondered.

"You don't need the scorpion key to visit them," Doug said. The heads of all four keys were shaped like animals — yet another mysterious aspect of the Enchanted Emporium.

"For that matter, neither do you," I reminded him.

I threw the stone. It skipped seven times.

Splish-splash.

Doug looked for another stone without thinking about it. "You're perfectly right," he said, rummaging through the pebbles. "But I need the key to go to the meeting."

I narrowed my eyes at him. "What meeting?" I said, but I'd already guessed the answer before I'd even finished asking.

Doug turned red. "How about this, bro," he said. "Let's make a gentleman's agreement."

"We'd have to agree on something first, Doug," I snarled. "What meeting?"

He didn't answer my question. "I'm keeping the key for three," he said. I figured he meant three more days — over the weekend. "Then I'll give it back to you. I swear."

Doug found a second, perfectly flat rock and passed it to me. I squeezed it so hard that my fingers felt like they would break.

"What meeting are you talking about, Doug?" I said, pushing him.

He turned away from me, facing the direction he'd come from. "Three days and then it's all yours, okay?" he said.

Splish-splash.

I knew Mr. Lily had sent a letter to the other magic shopkeepers around the world, asking them to take a stand on Semueld Askell and his attacks. My guess was: the Lilys must've received the other families' replies.

"Is it the meeting of the seven families, Doug?" I said. "Is it finally set up?"

Doug started walking away. "Three days," he repeated.

"At least tell me what they said!" I growled.

"Who?" Doug asked.

"What do you mean, who?" I said. "The Lilys! What did they say about me attending?"

He stopped. "What do you want them to say, Viper?" he said. "That the meeting of the families is impossible without you?"

Doug's words cut me deeply. He realized it, but it was too late to take back what he had said. I wasn't needed at the Enchanted Emporium.

Splish-splash.

I turned my back and stared at the sea stubbornly.

"Listen, Finley," he said. "Aiby—"

"Don't talk to me about her!" I shrieked.

"But I'm going to," Doug said. "When I asked you if you liked Aiby Lily, you said, 'Me? That girl? No way!'"

I clenched my fists. I had said that, it was true. But I'd lied, of course.

"Is that true or not?" Doug asked.

I don't know why, but I just couldn't bring myself to say it to him. "I like Patches," I muttered.

I picked up a stone that looked flat and tried to skip it across the surface. It sank into the sea.

"And where are you having this meeting?" I asked without looking at him.

"Nuh-uh," Doug replied enigmatically.

"'Nuh-uh' what?" I asked.

When I turned around, he was too far away for me to hear his answer. I just heard that strange splashing in the background that had seemingly punctuated our discussion.

The waves were majestic and cold. They skimmed indifferently across the pebbles, making them roll atop each other with a gravelly hum.

Splish-splash.

"What the heck is that noise?!" I said to myself.

I followed the noise to a puddle of briny water formed by a wave that had gone farther up the shore than the rest. A little shadowy thing was trapped in it. It thrashed its tail in the shallow water.

I smiled and leaned down to pick it up and throw it back into the sea. But the creature squirmed out from my hands and landed on the pebbles. With two quick strokes of its tail, it skipped across the pebbles and dove into the sea.

"You're welcome," I said. Right then I saw a tiny, shiny object in the same puddle. At first I thought it was a shard from a bottle or a piece of metal. But as I kneeled down and picked it up, I realized it was a tiny pocket mirror with a silver frame.

Chapter
THREE

MAN TO MAN,
THINGS UNSAID,
& THE DARK

The next morning, my father drove me into town in his van. I could sense he had something to tell me. He asked me twice if I was comfortable, which is what made it obvious since he'd never cared before.

My dad never really talked much, so it wasn't like we spent time chatting. When we were forced to converse, we did it as quickly and directly as possible so we could get back to important things, like fishing, shearing sheep, or going for a ride in the boat.

"Are you comfortable?" he asked for the third time.

The van's suspension had been shot for years. You could feel every pothole shake the seat all the way to your belly button. Patches was balanced on my legs,

hoping I'd open the window so he could put his head outside and feel his ears blow wildly in the wind.

"I'm fabulous," I said, keeping my eyes straight ahead. I knew that if our eyes met, my dad would attack me with a conversation he felt we needed to have.

We went silent for a few more turns. But when the first houses in Applecross loomed on the horizon, my father took a deep breath and said, "Listen, Finley . . . this business about that girl . . ."

"What business? What girl?" I asked.

"You know what I'm talking about," he said.

"No, I don't," I said.

After I'd returned from the beach the previous evening, I threw the puppet Aiby sent me over to Patches, telling him he should go bury it.

"I know it's not an easy thing," my father said, "but I need to talk to you, man to man."

In my experience with man-to-man conversations with my father, more words were spoken than in our normal conversations but less was actually said.

"You're old enough now that you've figured out some things on your own," my dad said. "As for the other stuff, well . . . it's better to ask your father instead of . . ."

I tried to help him out. "Instead of Doug?" I asked.

Camas McPhee looked at me. "I wasn't thinking of

Doug specifically," he said. "Just anyone who might fill your head with bad ideas." He brought the van to a stop. "Listen, Finley, it's a very easy thing to fall in love. But afterwards is when the problems begin."

Wow, I thought. *My father really wants to have a conversation.*

"Think of your mom and me," he continued. "We've been together for twenty years now." He hesitated. "You understand, right?"

I shrugged.

"All of us, as kids, end up with a crush on some pretty girl," my dad said. "Or even one who's not so pretty, for that matter."

"Dad, Aiby is incredibly —"

"Just let me speak," my dad interrupted. "I didn't mean that this friend of yours, Aiby, isn't pretty."

You better not have, I thought.

"What I want to tell you, son, is . . ." he trailed off.

"Dad," I began, but no words came.

Man-to-man conversations are not like actual discussions where one person speaks and the other asks questions. They're more like a nation's state of the union address: the person talking feels like his back is covered by thousands of other people who think just like him. Not coincidentally, the listener is usually much younger than the speaker.

My dad started up the car again and drove onward. For the next ten minutes, my father talked about girls and I listened. He talked about having crushes. He said when you're very young, as I was, relationships can seem much more complicated than they really are. And he said a few more things that had clearly come from my mother's lips. Even so, I appreciated the effort he made to see it through. In the end, visibly exhausted, he pulled the van up to Reverend Prospero's rectory.

"Do you understand what I mean, Finley?" he asked.

I nodded without saying anything. What was the point? He had just told me that my relationship with Aiby wasn't that big of a deal, and how could I argue with him? I couldn't tell him about how I'd defeated a stone giant who loved riddles, or about the forest spirit who wanted to steal my soul. If I told him about diving head first into the reef to see if I could cross between worlds, he'd probably have me committed to an asylum. Perhaps most kids my age did think things were bigger and scarier and more serious than they really were, but my situation was different.

Then again, maybe it really wasn't all that different.

I started to get out of the van, but then hesitated. I put Patches down. "Can I ask you something, Dad?"

He turned red, undoubtedly imagining the worst of all possible questions. "Of course," he said.

"How old were you when you met Mom?" I asked.

"About the same age as you," he said softly. "Maybe a year older, more or less."

"And back then, if you'd known someone else really liked Mom . . . and perhaps this other person was your friend, but he was playing dirty to take her away from you . . . what would you have done?"

He thought about that for a moment, seemingly relieved I hadn't asked him about the birds and the bees. "Well, it would depend if she —"

"Tell me the truth," I interrupted.

"Man to man?" he asked.

"Man to man," I said.

"You won't say a word to your mother?" he asked.

"Not a single one," I vowed.

My father chuckled. "I would have given him a good beating," my father admitted. "Or at least I would've tried to."

For the first time in days, a large smile spread across my face. "Thanks, Dad," I said. I walked around to the back of the van and grabbed my bike.

He left again, clearly satisfied with his work. Meanwhile, I shuffled to the rectory as slowly as possible, dreading whatever new task Reverend Prospero had in store for me.

★ ★ ★

29

"Cataloging rocks?" I repeated, holding the gigantic book he passed me.

"Exactly, son," Reverend Prospero replied. He seemed even larger and more imposing than usual, with his fiery eyes and the voice of a hurricane. "A professor friend of Mr. Everett is doing research on rock formations along the entire northwest coast of Scotland. He needs volunteers to take samples."

"And I'm that volunteer," I said.

"I thought it would be something interesting for you to do," Prospero replied. "All you need to do is go to these places that are marked." He showed me a map with fifty or so places noted with a red marker. "Bring a shovel and a few other digging tools with you." He pointed to a backpack filled with gardening equipment. "And compare the rocks with the catalog you have in your hands." I leafed through the huge book. It had all kinds of rocks with the names in Latin. "When you find one, put an X next to it in the catalog."

I saw out of the corner of my eye that the sites to be inspected included Reginald Bay, where the Lilys had reopened the Enchanted Emporium.

"That's fine with me, Reverend," I said, pointing at Reginald Bay. "As long as you never go there again."

Reverend Prospero looked at me, considering his

30

response. Just like with my father, a good part of our communication was nonverbal. He knew that I knew and I knew that he knew. But neither of us knew enough to ask the other what he knew.

It was complicated.

"That seems like a good idea to me, Finley," he finally said. "Much better for everyone, in my opinion." He marked a big red X on the Enchanted Emporium.

"Can I start right away?" I asked.

"At your leisure," the reverend replied. "The rocks have been waiting for you for a few million years. No harm in keeping them waiting a little longer."

I squinted at the reverend's attempt at a joke, checked the contents of the backpack, slung it over my shoulders, and took the map. The reverend accompanied me outside.

"Reverend?" I asked before saying goodbye.

"Yes?" he said.

"What was it like when the Others took you to the other side?" I asked.

His eyes flickered involuntarily. "Dark," was all he said.

I left.

Chapter
FOUR

STONES,
BONES, &
SECRETS

I decided to start at the dam, the rough cement barrier between the two mountains behind Applecross. The location was far enough away from everyone and everything that I knew I'd be alone, at least. All I could see, besides the hairpin curves in the single road that slid down into our valley, were rocks. Rocks, bushes, lichen, and more rocks.

The harder I tried to not think of either Doug or Aiby, the more my mind wandered back to them — like a dog with a bone, my dumb brain just wouldn't let go.

"Which is a great way to put it, right, Patches?" I said to my dog.

I got to work. It was slow and tedious. Up to that point, I'd thought that campers were the weirdest beings

on the planet, but that was only because I hadn't met any geologists. What could they possibly find so interesting about the fact that there were more yellowish rocks than bluish one at the dam?

"Maybe geology is a form of punishment for people who did something terrible in a former life," I suggested to Patches.

At school, they explained that Indians believed in something called reincarnation. That meant when you died, you were reborn in a different form. Maybe that's why cowboys shot Indians without worrying about it. Or maybe those were other Indians?

"Ignorance is bliss, Patches," I said, slightly ashamed at my lack of knowledge. "Ignorance is bliss."

I mean, you're always better off not knowing. I wished I hadn't known that Aiby had come to Applecross, or that Semueld Askell had arrived too. I wished I didn't know about the meeting of the shopkeeper families, and that Doug would attend it in my place.

I should have felt less foolish than I did. Only three days before, I had been thrilled to discover there was a passage on one of the islands that led to the Hollow World, a place where magical beings lived, where magic leaked into our world. Now those events seemed far away, as if someone else had experienced them.

"Three days," I muttered, stumbling over rocks to catalog the ones that were higher up. "I should just leave the key with Doug and stay ignorant forever!"

Mid-morning, I was hit by a wave of hunger. I opened the lunch I bought at the only pub in Applecross and split my bread and ham with Patches equally. As I munched, I continued to torment myself with worries.

Perhaps I should just tell everyone the crazy things I've seen, I thought. *But how could I even explain them?*

I sighed. "I guess if we always knew what to say, then we'd all talk like books," I said. Patches looked at me. "And then we'd have to say goodbye to surprises, right?"

Patches agreed, as always.

Somehow or other, the day passed by. It was time to go home, but I wanted to see Doug again about as much as I wanted to cut off my little finger. Instead of riding it, I tiredly pulled my magic bicycle all the way home.

When I finally got home an hour later, Mom told me that Doug wasn't there. For some reason, it felt like I'd really cut off that finger.

"Where'd he go?" I asked.

"He left early this afternoon," she said. "He looked everywhere for you."

"Imagine that," I muttered. "And when's he coming back?"

"Sunday," she replied.

I quickly counted the days of the week in my head. *Friday, Saturday, Sunday,* I thought. *That's why he needed the three days he had asked me for. Three days away from home, far away from Applecross . . .*

"But where on earth are they having that meeting?" I wondered aloud.

"What meeting?" my mom asked.

"I don't know, Mom," I replied. "But I'm going to find out."

I went up to Doug's room and closed the door behind me so my mom wouldn't think about following me. I opened the closet and an unbearable cloud of mint aftershave hit me in the face.

I groped through Doug's jackets until I found what he'd hidden at the bottom: a Closet Skeleton.

I draped it out the window the way Aiby had taught me to do, bathing it in the light for a bit. Then I told it, "I want to know where Doug went."

The skeleton's jaw creaked a little before it spoke. "He went to the Enchanted Emporium, where the others were waiting to leave," the skeleton said. Its raspy, hissing voice was not pleasant at all.

"Which others?" I asked.

"I don't know."

"Where were they headed?" I asked.

"I have no idea."

"Come on, talk!" I said.

"Your brother spent the whole morning deciding what to wear so that he'd be sure to make a good impression. His Knicks jersey was too tight and his hat was missing."

"I know," I admitted.

The skeleton in the closet looked at me. Apparently, he had a knack for sniffing out bad behavior, probably from having absorbed so many people's wicked thoughts.

"And?" I asked.

"He was worried about you."

"Why?" I asked.

"Because he didn't want you to worry."

"How clever of him," I said.

"He also wrote you a letter."

"Bah!" I snarled.

I grabbed the skeleton and tossed it back into the closet without even a word of thanks. Just as I left Doug's room, I found myself face to face with my mom.

"Would you mind explaining to me what's going on with you and your brother, Finley?" she asked.

"It's simple, Mom," I said. "Doug and Aiby are getting married."

Mom's face scrunched up. I took advantage of her confusion to slip past her into my room.

Doug had left the note in the middle of my bed, but it wasn't from him. Even at a distance I could recognize Aiby's handwriting on the envelope, as well as the golden words that shifted depending on the writer's thoughts.

Open me, please, it read.

When I snatched the envelope and prepared to crumple it up, the letters shifted to read: *You can't do everything on your own, Finley. Read me!*

That was just too much. It made me want to tear the envelope into pieces. Instead, I threw it into the corner of my room with the writing side down so I couldn't see it.

Patches sniffed it with interest, then barked.

My mom appeared in the doorway. "What made you say something like that to me?" she asked.

"I don't know," I said. "Doug and I have been fighting."

"That's obvious," she said calmly. "What isn't obvious, however, is why Doug seemed so disappointed he couldn't say goodbye to you."

I shrugged my shoulders and pretended to be interested in something outside the window. "It'll pass," I muttered.

That night seemed like it would never end.

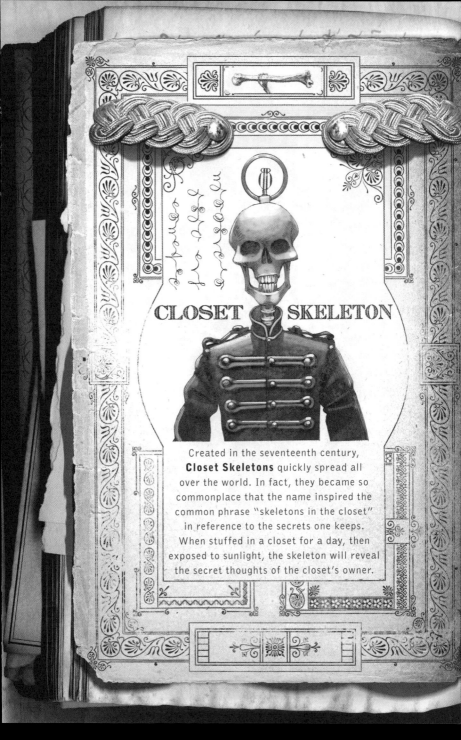

CLOSET SKELETON

Created in the seventeenth century,
Closet Skeletons quickly spread all
over the world. In fact, they became so
commonplace that the name inspired the
common phrase "skeletons in the closet"
in reference to the secrets one keeps.
When stuffed in a closet for a day, then
exposed to sunlight, the skeleton will reveal
the secret thoughts of the closet's owner.

BRAINS,
BRAWN, &
INTUITION

I woke up with my joints aching and two dark half-moons under my eyes. When Patches spotted me, he jumped on top of my chest to lick my face. He seemed heavy. I pushed him away as best I could, angered by his irrepressible happiness.

I struggled to gather the strength to lift off the covers and get out of bed. "How can you dogs be so happy every single morning?" I asked him.

I felt something strange beneath my feet. The envelope with the changing letters.

This time, the golden letters read, *It's important, Finley.*

"Don't try to enchant me," I said and kicked it under my bed.

I ruffled Patches' ears and went into the bathroom. My face was greenish-yellow. I tried rubbing my face with cold water, then hot water, but neither helped.

When I went back to look at myself in the mirror, I jumped back with fright. For an instant, I saw a face that wasn't mine staring back at me. But then it was gone.

I sighed. It wasn't the first time I'd seen odd things in the mirror when I was especially tired. Once I saw the face of my dead grandmother, whom I remembered almost nothing about other than the fact that she had read bedtime stories to me.

I brushed the mirror with my fingertip, leaving marks behind. Then I went downstairs.

I dragged myself around the kitchen, looking for something to shut up my stomach. "Do you want a ride in the van?" my father asked.

I said no, that I would go to work by bike. I made every effort to be vague about what I would be doing and where I would be going. I felt a manic urge to be completely out of reach.

"Cataloging rocks, huh?" was all my father said about my new assignment. "Reverend Prospero told me you're a smart kid, you know."

"He doesn't seem to think so," I replied, swallowing a handful of cereal.

★ ★ ★

I hopped off my bike at the last curve before the dam. My legs were screaming in pain, as if I had spent the whole night pedaling instead of sleeping. I walked my bike for a while.

I only got back on the seat when I heard a car approaching. I didn't want anyone to see me struggling.

Of course, it was the red van that belonged to Jules the mailman. He was driving along the hairpin turns — right in the middle of the road.

When he saw me, Jules slowed to a stop and lowered the window. "Everything okay, McPhee?" He shouted. "Need a lift?"

"No, thanks," I answered, giving him an overly enthusiastic thumbs-up sign. "I'm fine. And how are you?"

Jules laughed and told me he was delivering packages of books to everyone in the whole town. He was getting all the addresses confused. "But you know what they say," he concluded. "If you don't have brains, you'd better have brawn."

I stared blankly at him.

"Are you really okay, McPhee?" Jules asked. "You look as yellow as a stale French fry."

"I'm doing fine," I replied.

He shrugged and sped off. It's true that men communicate like no other living species. That is to say: badly.

★ ★ ★

Cataloging rocks was an absurd job. They were simultaneously all the same and all different. There was a little bit of red and a little bit of black in all of them. And a little bit of yellow, too.

Colored rocks were fine by me, though. I mean, as long as they weren't a part of a stone giant, I didn't care what colors or shapes they were.

I circled the entire basin and marked a great number of X's in the catalog, wondering who really needed this data. But the more I worked, the less I thought about, which was a good thing.

About mid-afternoon, I decided I'd finished working in that area. As I crossed the dam, I stopped to look down. The dam was gray and narrow like a long knife. It felt old and lonely, like an old tombstone, its writing eroded by wind and rain.

"Here lies Finley McPhee," I said gloomily.

Something white darted right at my face. I ducked, narrowly avoiding a collision.

"Stupid seagull!" I yelled. Patches barked at it, too.

It flew below the dam, completed a large circle, and

came back to aim its beady eyes and pointy beak at me. Then it dive-bombed me again. The seagull passed an inch away from my ear. Its claws skimmed my shoulder. Patches was barking fiercely at it now.

I shook my fist at the pest. "What are you doing?" I yelled.

Then I noticed that the seagull hadn't come alone. A whole flock was gliding over the water and shrieking their manic cries. A moment later, they were darting crazily around us.

I cursed at one, dodged another, and hit a third bird with the back of the rock catalog. Patches yelped and hopped up, trying to bite their wings.

I had no idea what was going on, but I didn't have the time to wonder. I ran to my bike with my hands protecting my head. The swirl of seagulls followed me, pinching me with their beaks and tugging on my shirt.

"Ow! Ow!" I screamed with every step. I was in an absolute panic — and being pecked from all sides.

While defending myself with the catalog, I tried to remember where I had left the backpack with its tools. I gave up when one of the seagulls pinched my butt.

The seagulls' fury died down when I reached my bicycle. Only then did I begin to understand. Most of the seagulls looked alike, but the one that was waiting for me on the handlebars of my bike was the gull from Reginald Bay who guarded the Enchanted Emporium. I recognized him from his wounded leg and held-down wing. Patches growled at him, a ritual of his ever since the first day they'd met.

The seagull shrieked. I don't know any other way to describe the harsh, guttural cry it produced. It shrieked again, then pecked at my bike's handlebars.

"Hey, sack of feathers, leave it alone!" I said.

The seagull's black eyes stared into mine. It puffed up its feathers as if it were trying to intimidate me as the other gulls circled above us like annoying vultures.

The seagull tilted its head at me. It deflated its feathers and pecked at the frame of my bike again. It seemed to be trying to tell me something.

"What do you want?" I asked.

Another bird glided in between us, and the old seagull let out a reproachful cry as if to say it didn't need help.

I swung my leg over my bicycle and sat on the seat. "You want me to follow you, don't you?" I asked.

The seagull dropped off the handlebars and backed away cautiously. Patches growled at it. It beat its wings, rising from the ground for a moment.

"I'll take that as a 'yes,'" I said. What can I say, I have

an instinct for these kinds of things.

"Did something happen to Aiby?" I asked.

The old seagull let out a sharp, shrill screech that reminded me of fingernails on a blackboard . . . or my mom's voice after I tracked mud all over the living room.

That's a yes, I thought. *An agitated one.*

The seagull flew into the air and glided away like a paper airplane. I pedaled in a frenzy to keep pace. "I'm coming, Aiby!" I said.

Chapter
SIX

SIGNS,
SUITCASES, &
PHOTOS

I pedaled, following the old gull in the lead as the others darted around me. The old gull flew straight while the others constantly swirled and plunged. They shepherded me along, barely brushing the spokes of the bike with the tips of their wings. I sensed urgency and pedaled harder.

We went back up the last turns in the road and plunged down the other side as the bay and the islands appeared on the horizon. Bike wheels spun furiously as the seagulls flew majestically toward the sea. We turned north along the coastal road, which I knew like the back of my hand. Then we came to the forest where Mr. Lily's trees had magically grown in a single night. But when we reached the sign with the shifting arrow, I stopped. I'd promised myself I'd never return to the Emporium.

The seagulls flapped above me, screeching. I watched them coast beyond the line of trees and descend into the valley of white stones that surrounded the Enchanted Emporium. The air quivered with menace. Patches panted at my feet.

I looked at my dog. His watery eyes seemed incredibly wise. "You're right," I said. "I'll break my promise. Just this once." He barked in response.

A moment later, I rounded the bend of the white path at the summit above Reginald Bay. I discovered I wasn't alone. In front of the Lilys' red house was a Japanese car with one door open.

Meb's already here, I thought. I pedaled faster.

One after another, the gulls grew quiet and glided above the white stones like sentinels.

As soon as she heard my bicycle racing across the gravel, Meb came out of the Enchanted Emporium. She was clearly upset. She had dark circles under her bright, pretty eyes and her hair was disheveled.

I skidded to a stop. "What happened?" I asked her between breaths.

"I don't know," she said. "The gulls just led me here."

Hanging from a chain outside the door of the Enchanted Emporium was a traditional Shifting Sign, which for other stores only had two sides: *Open* and

Closed. The Emporium's version, of course, had other possibilities, such as *Half-open, Staff at Sea, Knock Very Loudly: Music at High Volume, Push, Pull, Go Away, Please Change Clothes Before Entering, Place Swords in the Appropriate Vase, Please Leash Your Hippogriffs . . .* and so on and so forth.

In beautiful golden letters, the front of the sign hanging outside the door read: *We are in big trouble.* I flipped it over. The back read: *Please come rescue us.*

Meb pointed at the seagulls. "I think that's why they called us here," she whispered.

I knew that the Reginald Bay gulls were the Lily family's animal protectors, but I had no idea they could read. "Now what?" I asked.

"Now I think we should do something," Meb said, entering the shop.

I followed her. Without my key, the only way for me to enter was if she invited me in like a regular customer. As I crossed the threshold, goose bumps popped up all over my skin.

In the first room there was a long, antique wooden counter where hundreds of transactions had taken place. Its surface was worn by years of signatures, scratches, and spills.

A brass hotel-style bell sat on the counter. A sign next

to it read: *Ring in case of problems. Will respond as soon as possible. We do not exchange merchandise without a standard certificate of magic. We do not accept checks. - The Enchanted Emporium Staff*

The rest of the place was strangely empty. The items that were usually kept behind the counter had been put away before the Lilys' departure. The floor had been swept and there was a delicate scent of lavender in the room. After asking a few questions, I realized that Meb had also been kept in the dark about the details of their trip.

"Locan —" Meb began. "I mean, *Mr. Lily* just told me they wouldn't be in Applecross at the end of the week."

I nodded. I knew even less than that. "Should I ring the bell?" I asked her.

She nodded. "Ring it."

Ding! The door to the rear area of the store opened.

We crossed through a curtain of gently swaying glass beads that cast pleasantly flickering patterns into the living room. Aiby and her father spent part of each day reading and studying matters of magic there. It was covered from floor to ceiling with red wooden shelves filled with multicolored books and strange objects. I noted a marching toy soldier, a silver sack with smoke billowing out of it, and a typewriter that tapped keys on its own. Next to the only window was a tiny desk with a heavy, leather-bound book in the center: the *Big Book of Magical Objects*.

Meb took a quick look at the book, then faced the center of the room. "Everything seems in place here."

Two suitcases sat side by side next to the sofa. Both of them were old and had brass stamps and buckles. The leather was marked up from years of travel. The darker of the two suitcases belonged to Locan Lily. The lighter one was Aiby's.

"So they never left," I muttered.

"No, I think they did," Meb replied. "These are Stay-at-Home Suitcases."

"What?" I asked.

"They're double suitcases," Meb explained. "You take one with you and leave one at home. If you realize you've forgotten something during your trip, you can call home and ask someone to put it in the suitcase."

"And you'll find it in the other one?" I guessed.

"Exactly."

We examined the suitcases and tried to open them, but neither of us could.

"Now what?" I asked.

She shrugged. "I have no idea what to do in this situation."

I moved away from the *Big Book of Magical Objects* in the hopes that she wouldn't ask me to use it.

"Could you go and check the *BBMO*?" Meb asked.

I sighed and approached the desk with some discomfort. I tried to pick up the *BBMO*, but Meb reminded me that the book couldn't be removed from the surface of the desk. I had to read it there.

Rats, I thought. *Another reason to hate this book.*

The *BBMO* was written entirely in Incantevole, a magic language with letters that danced around the page like tadpoles in a pond. Whoever knew how to read Incantevole saw the letters form simple words and notes. Anyone who didn't know how to read Incantevole would only see scribbles and scrawls. The book had illustrations as well, but they were useless if you couldn't read the words next to them.

"Stay-at-Home Suitcases, right?" I asked, stalling. Meb didn't know I couldn't read the language. I mean, a few words were clear to me. I could put together complete sentences here and there, but not enough to really understand anything complicated.

Meb examined the stickers on the suitcases. "This old tag reads: 'In case of malfunction, contact Stay-at-Home Inc., In-Room Travel Agency, Vienna.' There's also a phone number listed."

"Wouldn't Aiby and her father have a normal phone with them?" I asked.

"Technology and magic have never gotten along well," Meb said. "Don't even try to talk to Locan about computers and televisions because he'll ask you to leave the room. It's almost worse than talking to him about religion."

It seemed bizarre to me that the Lilys would bicker with the cable guy, Seamus, or Reverend Prospero, but I didn't ask any more questions.

I flipped through the pages and found the drawing of the suitcases. There was a piece of paper attached to the description of how they worked. It was fastened with a little droplet of glue — just enough to keep it in place when leafing through the book. The letters in Incantevole danced sluggishly before my eyes.

"I found something," I muttered. "This handwritten note reads: 'Look for my Carbon Copy Diary.' I think it's a message from Aiby, but what is a Carbon Copy Diary?"

I leafed through the *BBMO* toy the entry. The Carbon Copy Diary was a travel notebook with white pages and a document pocket in the back, held closed by a thick black elastic band. Like the suitcases, the notebooks also worked in pairs. You carried your diary with you while traveling and wrote in it, inserted photos, and created sketches, and then all of it was instantly transferred to the copy that was safe in your room.

Of course the *BBMO* gave no indication of where Aiby's diary could be found. Aiby's letter from the day before came to mind. I suddenly wished I'd not been too stubborn to read it.

"If we want to have a chance of finding this Carbon Copy Diary, we should split up," Meb said.

The Lilys had a habit of scattering everything important, which tended to create a long, personalized treasure hunt — as if other people had nothing better to do than solve their little puzzles. It was an effective way to thwart thieves of magical objects, sure, but it was a hassle to everyone else.

So we split up. Meb went to look for Aiby's Carbon Copy Diary on the main floor while I went upstairs for the first time. I didn't have the slightest idea of what was up there. The staircase was red like the rest of the house and a multicolored rug was draped across the steps. They creaked as I ascended, making me feel a little like an intruder without the Lilys there. I was more than a little nervous that I might run into an unexpected trap.

Patches followed me, sniffing each step noisily. A large number of black-and-white photos lined the staircase wall. Most of them were shots of Aiby and her father. One showed Aiby with her dark hair pretending to pout. Another showed Locan Lily sitting in front of a table laden with food. Another pictured Aiby wearing a white shirt, pointing enthusiastically at something outside the picture frame. The last one displayed Mr. Lily leaning over a twisted tree trunk that he seemed to be animating with his hands in the air.

Like a puppeteer, I thought.

The highest photos along the staircase were of people I didn't know. They seemed much older than the others. One showed a man with a strange hat and an ominous look on his face. Another showed a smiling couple wearing ridiculous bathing suits from another time.

I recognized some photos taken from the opening of the Emporium that summer. I was even in one of them, next to Aiby, but I was looking in the other direction. I touched it lightly with a finger. It seemed so strange to find it there, and I wondered who might have taken it. Then I heard Meb moving the furniture around and opening boxes down below in search of the diary, and I remembered what I was supposed to be doing.

I climbed the last steps of the steep staircase and reached a landing with four doors. The first door led to a small bathroom that had a large bathtub with lion's paws. Piles of books and magazines were on the floor. From the window, you could see the trees at the top of the cliff.

Patches and I didn't move past the doorway. The diary was unlikely to be in there.

The second door was closed. A pensive gargoyle was balanced on the door handle. It held a sign between its paws that read: *Don't even think about it.*

"Whatever you say," I said, moving on.

The third door was held open with an Oriental cushion. Aiby's name was written on the door with letters made of differently colored wood. The sensation of being an intruder increased, so I turned away.

I examined the final door that was right next to Aiby's. It was slightly ajar, and it seemed to be guarded by a doorstop in the shape of a little dachshund made of red, white, and gray wool. Patches had already begun to sniff it in curiosity. I, however, had my eyes fixed on the sign hanging from the doorjamb. It read: *Hell is other people.* Many years later, I would discover it's a quotation by a French writer named Jean-Paul Sartre.

Through the crack, I caught a glimpse of a tiny office with two old wooden desks pushed up next to each other. I gently pushed the door open and noticed a bookcase overflowing with notebooks, a deep-sea diving helmet, a lily contained in a crystal ball hanging from the window, and an old globe with a golden base. But what struck me more than anything else there was a computer screen wrapped up with dozens of pieces of scotch-tape and paper like a mummy.

For a moment, I thought Aiby and her father had finally bought something modern. But when I got closer I saw that the computer was covered in dust and realized it must have been packed up many years earlier.

On a shelf in the library, I noticed a photo in a silver frame. It showed Aiby and her father with a shorthaired woman wearing a pair of gold-rimmed glasses and a shabby gray dress. She had one hand on Aiby's shoulder and the other arm around Mr. Lily's waist, which made me think it had to be Aiby's mom. Aiby and Mr. Lily barely spoke about her. It was like the circumstances of her death were still painfully present in their memories.

"Have you found anything?" Meb called from below.

"Maybe!" I lied. Then I quickly left the disturbing office and went right into Aiby's room.

Patches was still trying to impress the doorstop. "Patches, it's not a real dog," I explained to my indefatigable friend.

Then again, in the Enchanted Emporium, you never knew.

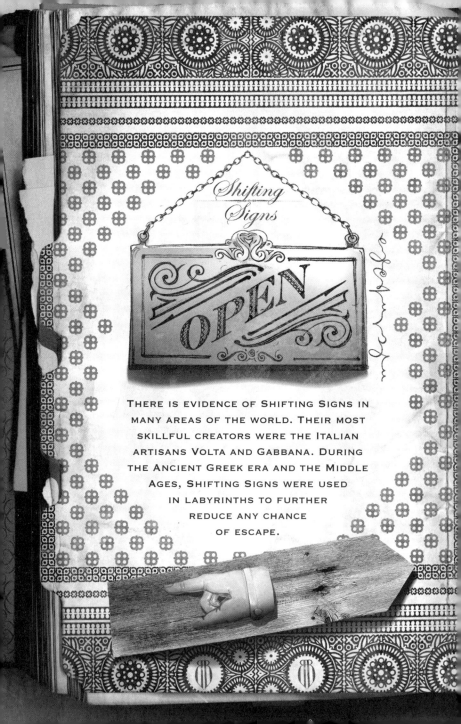

Shifting Signs

OPEN

THERE IS EVIDENCE OF SHIFTING SIGNS IN
MANY AREAS OF THE WORLD. THEIR MOST
SKILLFUL CREATORS WERE THE ITALIAN
ARTISANS VOLTA AND GABBANA. DURING
THE ANCIENT GREEK ERA AND THE MIDDLE
AGES, SHIFTING SIGNS WERE USED
IN LABYRINTHS TO FURTHER
REDUCE ANY CHANCE
OF ESCAPE.

LOCKS,
A DIARY, &
TALKING FURNITURE

I entered Aiby's room on tiptoes, stopped on the yellow rug, and looked around. There were thousands of things in it. Aiby's bed was just a mattress resting on the floor. Next to it was a nightstand made from an old armchair. Dozens of adhesive stars clung to the ceiling. A small family of wooden penguins swung gently in the air. A copper candelabra with twelve arms sat next to a dream catcher with silver feathers.

There was no wardrobe or dresser — in its place was a large bookcase with folded shirts, sweaters, and jeans in colorful stacks separated by books. There was a pair of sports medals (which is how I discovered that Aiby was a skiing champion) and drawings of animals hanging from the walls. And, impressively, one entire wall had been turned into a mirror, which Aiby had written on as if it were a blackboard.

A large window overlooked the bay. In the opposite corner from the mirrored wall stood a small desk with a roll-top that could be turned over and closed in on itself like the lid of a bread box. It seemed like the perfect place for putting a diary. The desk even had a tiny lock. Naturally I didn't have the key.

Meb came up the stairs and joined me. She agreed that this piece of furniture would be the first place to look.

"But how do we get it open?" I asked.

"Usually a desk's key is in a drawer," she said.

There were seven drawers — two on the sides over the legs, five where the top closed.

"Do you know which drawer it's in, too?" I joked, grabbing the handle of one of the drawers. Right away, I felt the normal magical tingling that I had learned to recognize as the presence of a magic spell.

"This is the Drawer of Magical Things," murmured the piece of furniture.

At the sound of the voice, Patches barked and his tail stood on end.

"A talking drawer . . . interesting," I commented. "I'm guessing you won't open on your own."

"Of course not," the piece of furniture added in a kindly voice. "I'm a Secretary. I don't let just anyone learn my secrets!"

I didn't take my hand off the handle. "May I at least ask what kind of secrets they are?" I ventured.

"Of course not," it said, still pleasant.

"I'm looking for Aiby's Carbon Copy Diary," I said.

"I know it well," the piece of furniture replied. "I have it right here, inside the Drawer of Places."

"And what would the Drawer of Places be?" I asked.

"You don't know?" the piece of furniture replied, apparently alarmed by my ignorance. "The Drawer of Places is behind the Flap of Time."

Hmm, I thought. *This thing likes to talk . . .*

I touched the lock. "Does that mean I should open this?" I asked.

"Careful with those fingers!" the desk cried. "You're tickling me!"

"Sorry," I replied. "Since I don't have the key, is there any other way to open the Flap of Time?"

"Sorry, the key is the only way," the desk said.

"And is the key inside one of these other drawers?" I asked.

"I can't tell you that!" the piece of furniture blurted out. "It's a secret and I'm a —"

"A Secretary, yes, I understand," I interrupted. "But if you can't tell me if the key's in one of your drawers . . . how do you know someone else didn't steal it?"

"I'm keeping it safe," the piece of furniture said proudly.

A-ha! I thought.

By now, I had a certain amount of experience dealing with magical objects. I let go of the small handle and tried to open the drawer next to it.

"This is the Drawer of Luck," the piece of furniture said right away.

It was locked, too. "Apparently I'm not lucky," I grumbled.

Meb whispered to me, "Do you want a hand?"

I signaled to her that I could manage this on my own.

Having found the third drawer locked as well, I asked, "What should I do to open you? All the drawers are locked."

"You just have to tell me the correct secret, and I'll let you open it," the piece of furniture answered.

"The correct secret?" I asked.

"Each drawer has its own secret," the secretary said.

Figures, I thought. I had to admit, it was a pretty great system for keeping drawers locked. Secrets protecting a diary presumably filled with secrets. I didn't have the slightest idea which secret would open it. So I guessed.

"Aiby's mom is dead," I said.

"That's certainly not a secret," the piece of furniture said.

"How am I supposed to tell you a secret if you then tell me it's not a secret because I know it, too," I grumbled.

"That's why I'm an excellent Secretary," the desk said proudly.

Other than possibly trying to force the drawer with something, I was out of ideas. I looked to Meb for help but she simply shrugged.

I decided to try to get more information out of it. "So you knew about Aiby's mom?" I asked.

"Everyone knows about her," it responded.

It was right. But then what *was* the secret? My mom always said that there are no better secrets than the ones that everyone knows, whereas my father once said that three people can only keep a secret if two of them are dead. Neither perspective seemed particularly helpful.

"Last year I sealed the front door to school shut with glue and fishing wire," I said.

"So what?" the desk replied.

"Well, it's a secret," I said. "I never told anyone about it. There was some homework in math class that I skipped doing, too."

"That's a very nice secret," the piece of furniture admitted. "But it's *your* secret. You can use it to lock a drawer once you've opened it, but certainly not to open one that someone else has locked."

Do I even know any of Aiby's secrets? I wondered.

"Is a secret between two people valid?" I asked.

"Only if neither of them has ever told a third person," the piece of furniture said.

I had to use a secret that Aiby had only told me about, but I couldn't come up with anything. "I'm a fool," I muttered.

"That's not a secret," the Secretary retorted.

I frowned. "Aiby hates Incantevole," I said to the Drawer of Magical Items.

"Askell is Aiby's cousin," I tried on the Bad Memories drawer.

"I don't know how to iron," I said to the one for Magical Items.

"Not valid, not valid, and not valid!" the desk said proudly.

Maybe I have to reason this through differently, I

said to myself. Not with my head. Or rather, I shouldn't just reason with my head.

I grabbed the Drawer of Bad Memories and said, "Aiby likes Doug McPhee."

No luck. I tried the phrase on all the other drawers just to be safe. The last one I tried, the Drawer of Friends, creaked.

"Ahem, sorry," the Secretary explained. "I made a mistake."

I let out a big sigh of relief. Meg giggled. I blushed.

Patches stood up on his hind legs and leaned his front paws on my legs and tapped me with his nose to let me know he was getting bored. It was the same thing he did whenever Aiby and I were talking and he got jealous.

"You know something, Patches? You gave me an idea," I said to him, petting him with my free hand.

I whispered to the Drawer of Friends, "Aiby like Finley McPhee."

"Ta-dah!" the piece of furniture said, and the drawer slid open.

I couldn't help but grin.

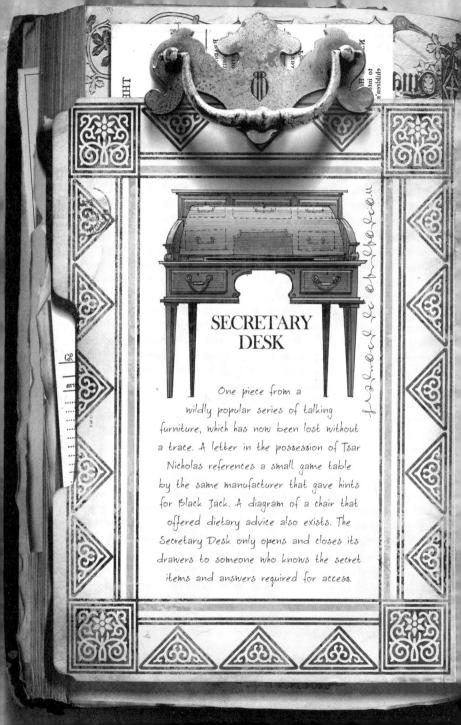

SECRETARY DESK

One piece from a
wildly popular series of talking
furniture, which has now been lost without
a trace. A letter in the possession of Tsar
Nicholas references a small game table
by the same manufacturer that gave hints
for Black Jack. A diagram of a chair that
offered dietary advice also exists. The
Secretary Desk only opens and closes its
drawers to someone who knows the secret
items and answers required for access.

Chapter
EIGHT

DIARIES,
SECRETS, &
DOLLS

I nside the Drawer of Friends was a swimsuit that I immediately recognized. (It was the one Aiby had worn the day I kissed her!) Beneath it was a picture of a wolf — and the little brass key I was looking for.

I opened the desk's roll-top and scanned through the items inside. There were pens, paper, a small golden anvil, a ball of amber with an insect in it, a necklace that jingled, and five little drawers. The one on the left was ajar. Inside it was a small black diary. The title page read: *Aiby's Carbon Copy Diary.*

I opened it. The first few pages had been torn out. The diary began with an entry from the day before, titled: *We're leaving, finally!*

Clipped to the first page was a ticket for a bus line called Incognito.

Below the ticket was a journal entry:

I'm excited about taking this trip and especially about seeing all the Others again. I wonder who they'll be and what they will tell us. Dad chose a magnificent place. If it weren't for Professor Everett, perhaps we would never have known that the library the Sunken Castle was so near Applecross. But we still left late, as usual for us. Dad insists it's impolite to be the last to arrive when you've organized a meeting, but I say not to worry about it.

The three Van de Maya sisters — April, May, and June — will definitely be there, confirming they'd left Flanders on Wednesday. Yuram Legba will come alone, which is a good thing since his last guest practically destroyed the hotel room. The Tiagos — Alejandro and Maria — will arrive together in their hot-air balloon. Teobaldo Scarselli promised to cook for everyone at the end of the meeting. He brought the ingredients for his unbeatable recipes with him. He said, "Although it's not true that you can't eat well in England, in Scotland, it's guaranteed." Two of the Moogleys will be there: that thug, Willard, and Tupper, whom I've never met because he was too young to join us when we went to New York to meet his uncle.

After arriving at the castle, Dad confirmed (for the umpteenth time) that the gifts we've prepared for the attendees

have already been delivered to the castle the library. When he finally saw Doug McPhee arrive, he breathed a sigh of relief. Luckily Finley wasn't coming, because then we would've left tomorrow.

At that point I closed the diary and passed it to Meb. "If you really want to read it, go ahead," I said. "I don't think I can stand it."

Meb skimmed through a dozen pages of entries, many of which were crossed out. Some pages had been torn out, and there were quite a few drawings.

When Meb reached the last page, she cried out, "My goodness!"

"My goodness what?" I asked.

"It says right here that Askell came to the meeting," Meb said.

"That's impossible!" I said. "Semueld Askell was a pillar of salt up until the other day! And he certainly wasn't invited to the meeting!"

"Nonetheless, it seems he went," Meb muttered. She leafed backward through the pages of the diary. "It says here that he stepped out from a mirror."

"How did he do that?" I asked.

Meb shrugged. "But two lines farther down the same entry, Aiby wrote a name: *Imagami.*"

"That's not the name of one of the magic shopkeeper

families," I said. "It tells us nothing."

We sat down on the floor next to each other. "What else did she write?" I asked.

"It's not very clear," Meb said. We read another of Aiby's entries:

Askell is dead serious, and he didn't come alone. My father senses great danger. I'm afraid. Mr. Tiago is worried, and so are April, May, and June, who haven't spoken for more than half an hour. The mood is tense. We told Semueld that his actions were ridiculous and dangerous and that no one had ever rebelled against the families in such a way. "The pact has changed," Askell replied. "The only way to avoid a revolt among the magical creatures is to surrender the Ark of the Passages to them." My father told Semueld that he was speaking nonsense. Askell was surly and sullen, and he just kept insisting that the Ark was in Applecross and guarded by the Enchanted Emporium. He said this meeting was a farce and that we Lilys were deceiving everyone.

My father asked Askell why we would keep the Ark hidden in the shop, and Askell shouted, "The same reason you always have! To control magic!" Then Legba asked Semueld why he wanted to find this mysterious Ark of the Passages. Askell said he'd been given the task by the Queen of the Others — a woman also known as Imagami. Legba asked if anyone had ever heard of Imagami, and everyone shook their heads. "She's not a Wizard, nor an Ancient, nor a Builder, nor even a Sleeping Queen! What does she want from us?" Legba added. Askell let out cackle.

Then Teobaldo Scarselli stepped in and said that "All the Askells are magic weapons sellers. And weapons sellers only know how to do one thing: prepare for war." Legba got to his feet and stared Askell in the face. "Are we at war?" he asked. "Don't be a coward — stand up and justify your actions! Are the families at war with this Imagami?" Askell smirked. "Yes, we're at war. And now you'll be locked up while the war rages!"

Meb and I exchanged worries glances. "Uh-oh," she whispered.

"Then they're trapped?" I said. "In here?"

We leafed through the other pages, but there was no explanation. At the bottom of another entry, however, were a few shocking sentences:

Finley, I beg you! If you read these pages, come to rescue us. You have to use the ticket I left for you to get to the Sunken Castle — before it's too late!"

Meb and I remained seated on the yellow rug in Aiby's room, staring at each other.

"Do we have a backup plan?" I asked after a particularly long moment.

Meb leafed through the diary, front to back. "Hmm," she said a short while later. "Do you know who this Angelica is?"

"No," I said. "Why?"

"Aiby wrote here that she feels like Angelica, one of the Sicilian Puppets," Meb said. "Angelica is the woman the two famous Paladins of France fought over. Aiby says that you and Doug are like Orlando and Rinaldo."

I blushed. "Anything else?" I asked.

Meb read from the entry: "'Luckily Angelica knows what should be done.'"

"Wait!" I cried out, remembering something from two evenings ago. "Angelica is the name of the puppet Doug gave me!"

Meb's eyes went wide. "And do you have her with you?" She asked.

"Well, no," I admitted. "Not . . . not exactly."

"What did you do with her, Finley?" Meb said, more of an accusation than a question.

I pointed at Patches. "I was furious! I gave the doll to Patches to bury," I said. "It's his fault!"

My trusty friend hid his head behind his paws. Meb put her head between her hands.

My shoulders slumped. "How badly did I mess up?" I asked.

"I don't know," Meb replied, pulling herself to her feet. "But it's possible you ruined our only plan B. Either way, we need to retrieve that puppet."

Chapter
NINE

ADVICE,
THE STARS, &
A TICKET

Meb sped toward my home in her little car. Upon arriving, we leapt out and ran to where Patches had buried Angelica.

I dug through the dirt, fist over fist. Thankfully, Patches hadn't bothered to bury her very deep — but before doing so, he had gnawed on her a bit. Angelica was still a beautiful wooden puppet, though, with blond hair, tin armor, and a terrifying temper.

"You lout," she yelled after spitting out a fair amount of dirt. "Now I'll bury you! You're all as cruel as beasts from the zoo!" She had a piercing, rhythmic voice — and an annoying habit of speaking in rhyme.

I covered Angelica's mouth and told Meb to go distract my parents. While the three of them sat and chatted on the porch while watching the stars, I snuck the puppet to my room and closed the door. I laid her on my bed and removed my hand from her mouth. She began waving her arms around and screaming orders like a banshee.

"Scamp!" she cried. "Lout! I hope you get gout!"

Getting Angelica to talk had been easy, but getting her to shut up was starting to seem impossible. Thankfully, Aiby had written instructions in the letter:

Finley,

I don't know how to express how terrible I feel right now, but I hope that one day you'll be able to understand. All I can tell you right now is that my father is very worried about you and thinks you in particular are in grave danger. If he's right, and the seagulls come to find you, ask Angelica what to do. To get her to speak, just turn her head to one side and say "Orlando!" to her. Then turn her head to the other said, and say, "Rinaldo!" I warn you that Angelica is not very polite, but she is conscientious. Tell her who you are and what you need her to do, then follow her instructions without question (which no one ever does since they think they can't learn anything from toys).

Please burn this letter after reading it.

- Aiby

I didn't burn it since it was summer and the fireplace

wasn't lit. Instead, I tore it into little pieces and placed them under my pillow. I peered out the half-open window. Meb was still chatting softly with my parents.

I sat down on the bed and picked up Angelica. "I'm Finley McPhee, Angelica," I said to the puppet. "Aiby and her father haven't returned. I believe they've been imprisoned by Semueld Askell."

"In jail! In a cell! Do not fail! She's your belle!" Angelica said. "Come now, and go! Don your anger, don't be slow! You're the hero, you're in the right! Have no fear, go win the fight!"

"What should I do?" I said, rubbing my temples.

"You'll be armed, don't be alarmed!" Angelica cried. "You'll have your gear, just look under here! Then make a wish!" I stared at her blankly. Under her breath, Angelica added, "Why'd we ever choose this fish . . ."

I frowned at the smart-alecky doll, then lifted the edge of the bed sheet. To my great surprise, I saw that someone had slipped two suitcases beneath my bed.

Doug, I realized.

They were Stay-at-Home Suitcases. Both of them had labels attached to them. They read:

FINLEY MCPHEE

ENCHANTED EMPORIUM

I pulled them out from under the bed and heard

something move inside. I clicked open the first suitcase's locks and opened it wide to find a pair of small boxes and one large bundle. On the inside of the lid, Aiby had written the names of three different magical objects:

Night Spectacles: Indispensable for when the darkness assails you.

Transmogrifier: Think of an animal you want to become and picture it in your head!

Lightning Launcher: Once you grasp it, it does everything else by itself.

In the first box, I found a pair of sunglasses with weird frames. The second box contained an engraved seal for marking wax. Inside the bundle of fabric, I found a sword with a silver hilt sheathed in a black scabbard.

"Wow!" I cried. I'd never seen such a beautiful handle. It was made from a lattice mesh as light as lace, and it had a purple stone set in the center. I gently slipped the sword out of its scabbard. It felt weightless in my hand. I contemplated the thin, white blade as it quivered ominously in the night. Along the side of the blade, several tiny, illegible letters shined in the starlight.

I slashed the air like a fencer. "This is quite a sword."

The *zing!* sound the blade made caused Patches to hide in the shadows. Even Angelica stared at me in awe. It felt like the sword had always been mine — and always would be. That's how it felt to hold the mighty Lightning Launcher.

I glanced at Angelica. "What should I do now, in your opinion?" I asked.

"What are you missing? What else do you want? Your spirit needs lifting! With heroes you'll jaunt! You have the ticket, the sword, and the letter. Someone with courage would be able to get her!"

I needed to stay calm as I was tempted to cut off her head. I knew I had to find the Sunken Castle — that much was clear. I made a mental list of the things I had that might help: I had Aiby's diary as well as her message asking for help, and I had the ticket for that strange bus line. I also had the suitcases — one of which I'd take with me, and the other I'd leave behind with Meb in case I ran into problems. But what else did I need?

I saw a silvery reflection on the table in my room. The tiny pocket mirror I'd found on the beach the day Doug left was reflecting starlight. I tossed it into the suitcase. I placed Angelica inside along with it, ignoring her protests. Then I tied some rope to both suitcases and lowered them out the window.

I dropped the rope down with the suitcases. I walked downstairs, left through the rear door, and circled the house to where I'd dropped the suitcases. Carefully, I loaded them into Meb's tiny car. Then I went back to the front porch and joined my parents and Meb.

The moonless night revealed a magnificent starlit sky. My parents were relaxed and staring up at the stars in silence. Meb looked at me, obviously wondering what the plan was. I gave her a thumbs-up got lost in the sea of stars along with my mom and dad.

Until that summer, Applecross had been the most boring town in all of Scotland. That all changed when the Lilys arrived. Now, even the most mundane things seemed interesting. But even at that moment, I was still naïve — I thought that only myself, Meb, Doug, and the Lilys knew anything about the magical world surrounding us. Had I paid more attention that evening, I would've noticed the poignant look my father gave my mother to indicate it was time for them to go to sleep so I could be alone with Meb.

The world seemed like a universe ripe for exploring, and I felt like its biggest hero.

Once I was sure my parents were far enough away, I quickly told Meb about the puppet and the two suitcases that I'd prepared in case they were needed.

"From what I can tell, the Lilys have the gift of foresight," I finished.

"And when do you plan to leave?" Meb asked.

"Right away, I'd say," I said. "I have no idea how long it takes to get to this Sunken Castle, but Aiby wrote that it wasn't very far away from Applecross."

Meb passed me the diary. "She called it a 'library' twice, but both times the word was crossed out."

I nodded. There were many words crossed out in that diary. I wondered if my name was one of them.

I pointed to the road leading to the village, just outside the gate to our farm. "Will you wait for me at the first turn?" I asked.

When Meb went back to her car, I patted Patches and asked him to be a good dog and wait outside for me. Then I closed the door carefully and went upstairs.

I slipped my pillows under the covers so it'd look like I was sleeping there. Then I wrote my parents a short note in case they saw through my not-so-clever ruse.

After I'd finished writing, I reread the note, crumpled it into a ball, and wrote a second one:

I have to go be a hero.

Don't worry about me. I'll come back as soon as possible.

Don't look for me (or Patches).

P.S.: I borrowed fifty bucks from Dad's wallet, just to be safe. I'll pay it back.

I left the note on my bed, climbed down from the window, and landed like a cat. I circled the house, proud of my stealthy escape.

Then my rascal of a dog barked at me. I pet him to keep him calm while we stayed still for a few minutes to make sure my parents hadn't woken up. After that, I ran down the path to the farm, tossed Patches outside the gate, climbed over it myself, and then jogged along the coastal road. Meb's car was waiting at the first turn. She had gotten out to gaze at the sea . . . and she was smoking.

"I didn't know you smoked," I said, standing by her.

"Neither did I," she said.

"Those things will kill you, you know," I said with a smirk.

Meb smiled. "Since when are you the responsible one?" she joked. She threw the cigarette on the ground and stamped it out with her foot. Then she caught my eye, picked it back up, and deposited it into the ashtray in her car. Both of us smiling, we hopped in her car, Meb started the engine and drove us along the Baelanch Ba.

We drank in the view from the coastal road. Neither of us spoke. Patches sniffed at the suitcases in the backseat. Eventually, we reached the crossroads for the Emporium. Meb stopped and we got out.

"What now?" Meb asked.

I opened Aiby's diary and pulled out the strange bus ticket. It had a logo of a tree with upside-down roots on it. I showed it to Meb.

"Any instructions?" Meb asked.

I pointed at the dotted line around the roots. A line of text read: *All aboard the Incognito Bus! For profound Journeys, tear here . . .*

"So tear it, then," Meb said.

"But it makes no sense," I said. "We should figure out what it does first."

Meb smiled. "What does Aiby always say about you needing answers?" she teased.

I nodded. With both hands, I tore the bus ticket in half. We waited. Naturally, nothing happened. "Maybe that's not how you're supposed to do it," I muttered.

"Or maybe it is," Meb whispered, pointing to the horizon.

I could barely see the headlights of a red London bus tottering toward us along the coastal road.

STAY-AT-HOME SUITCASES

949,287.

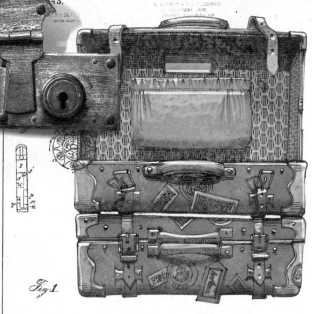

Fig. 1.

Fig. 6.

THESE SUITCASES WERE INVENTED BY A FORGETFUL
TRAVELER WHO WANTED TO HAVE ACCESS TO HIS
BELONGINGS WHILE HE WAS ABROAD. THEY ARE ALWAYS
SOLD IN PAIRS: ONE OF THE SUITCASES REMAINS AT
HOME WHILE THE OTHER STAYS WITH THE TRAVELER; IF
SOMETHING IS FORGOTTEN ON A TRIP, SOMEONE AT HOME
CAN SIMPLY INSERT THE OBJECT INTO THE SUITCASE AND
IT WILL INSTANTLY APPEAR INSIDE THE OTHER ONE. (IT
IS, HOWEVER, CONSIDERED INAPPROPRIATE TO USE
THEM TO SEND HOME SOUVENIRS.)

Witnesses:
Richard Sommes
Gustav W. Hora.

L. R. Pierce
J. A. Dischinger

ENCHANTED EMPORIUM

Inventors

by Geyer

Attorneys.

A BUS,
TIM, &
SMALL TALK

When the Incognito Bus neared us, its driver turned on the blinker and pulled over to the side of the road. Its destination sign read: *Finley McPhee.*

The driver opened the door and greeted me with a sharp nod. He was stocky, burly, and extremely hairy. A New York Knicks baseball cap sat on his head (which happened to my favorite basketball team — and Doug's).

"No animals on board," he said when he saw Patches.

"He's not an animal," I said. "He's my family member."

The man checked his book of regulations. He grunted, "Fine. I don't want any problems, okay?"

Patches and I reluctantly climbed aboard. The bus lurched forward with a jerk and a wheeze. I placed

Patches on the seat next to me and waved to Meb through the window. Her expressed made it clear she was just as worried as I was.

I caught the driver looking at me in the huge rearview mirror. "Do you know where we're headed?" I asked him.

He shifted gears. "You tell me," he said.

I turned around to check if anyone else was on the bus, but I saw only empty seats and little colored mirrors hanging from the windows. The floor gave off a sickly sweet smell.

I sighed. "Never mind," I said. "I was just trying to make conversation."

The driver tackled a turn in the road with a certain lightheartedness. Then he adjusted his cap and asked me, "First time?"

"Excuse me?" I asked.

"It's the first time you've taken this bus," he said.

"Y-yes," I said. "To be honest, I'm a little confused."

"That's normal," he said with an air of indifference. "Not many of your kind take this trip."

I sat in silence for a while. Without anything better to do, I opened Aiby's diary to look for advice. Right after the pages about the departure, Aiby had written down some remarks — that her father was quiet and clearly worried while Doug never shut up (which seemed to me to be pretty normal for both of them). She mentioned they had taken the Incognito Bus, but she gave no information about its grouchy driver or the trip's length.

This particular entry ended mid-sentence. *Aiby must have fallen asleep along the way,* I figured. *Talking to Doug for too long will do that to you.*

I flipped through the rest of the pages — the few that hadn't been torn out, anyway. In one entry, Aiby wrote: *The trials to get there are three. Discouraged you mustn't be. Only a true hero will pass and be free.*

Everything she wrote was interesting — at least to me. Especially her thoughts about other thoughts.

"I wonder why girls write these kinds of things," I wondered aloud, "but they never write where they are, what they're doing, or why they're doing it."

"Hey, who can say?" the driver said. "But rest assured that's just the way it is, old chap."

I picked up the notebook. "I mean, take this entry for example. She wrote twelve pages about her feelings!"

"It keeps her happy," the driver said.

Given my extensive experience of reading diaries (this being the only one), a magical bus driver's opinion seemed as good as anyone's. Besides, it couldn't hurt to find some common ground.

"I think you're right," I said. "My name's Finley. This little rascal here is Patches."

"Hullo," the driver said and tipped his cap. "I'm Tim. But everyone calls me Timmy."

"Pleased to meet you, Tim," I said.

He grunted. "The pleasure's mine," he said. "Do you mind if I put on a little music?"

"Anything you like," I said. Then I added, "Well, anything but ABBA."

"Hey, now we're talking," agreed Tim.

"No Justin Timberlake, either," I added.

"Finally someone who knows his stuff," Tim said.

Irish folk music filled the cabin. I knew it well. It was Villagers.

I was starting to like that bus. I leaned back and read some of the earlier pages of Aiby's diary, but the light inside the bus was dim and the scenery raced by. After a couple of pages, I started to feel nauseated.

I set the diary on my lap and yawned. A moment later, my head drooped. I decided that if I had to rescue Aiby, her father, all the shopkeepers, and possibly even Doug, then I might as well get some rest. I pulled the lever that was supposed to make the seat recline, but it wouldn't budge.

"Afraid it's broken, friend," Tim told me. Before

I could move to another seat, he added, "They're all broken, actually."

"You should get someone to fix them," I said sleepily.

"No point. They want it this way," Tim grunted. "The broken parts make the bus 'vintage.' It's part of the experience, you see: the tree-root ticket torn in half, the red London bus, the driver who's a little unsociable but also a little nice who reminds you of one of the fairy tales by the Brothers Grimm . . . "

"Hey, I didn't think that!" I lied.

"Actually, you don't seem like the others I've taken for rides," Timmy said. He nodded firmly, noisily blew his nose, and shifted gears with a rumble. "For all I know, you're straight out of a book written by Dr. Seuss."

I yawned. "Yeah, right," I said. "Dr. Seuss? Ha. More like H.P. Lovecraft." Another yawn. "Sorry if I fall asleep at some point."

"No problem, I'm used to it," the driver said. "In fact, thanks for the conversation, old chap."

Patches was a bundle of warm fur curled up next to me. "My pleasure," I said. "You know where to stop, right?"

Tim chuckled. "Of course!" he said. "We stop at the crossroads."

Those were the last words I heard.

Chapter
ELEVEN

MR. TOMMY,
THE HERO'S JOURNEY, &
A COADJUTOR

When I woke up, we had reached the crossroads. The bus engine was off and the door was open. A faint breeze came from outside, which made the little mirrors hanging from the windows jingle.

The bus driver was gone. I rubbed my eyes and looked around. "Tim, are you there?" I called out. "Mr. Tim? Timmy?"

I figured he must have gotten off to stretch his legs (or maybe we had a flat?), so I did the same. The bus's hood was warm to the touch, so we hadn't been stopped for very long.

Small stars shined in the sky. They seemed more distant than those I'd seen at my house. We were near a forest. Except for a streetlight shining right in the middle of a fork in the road, it was completely dark.

The driver said we would stop at the crossroads, I remembered.

Bus drivers usually don't vanish into thin air in the middle of the night, I thought. *He must be around here somewhere.*

"Tim?" I called out again. I circled the bus twice, then went back inside to check the upper level and between the seats, but I found nothing and no one. A light scent of mint aftershave filled the upper deck, which reminded me of Doug's closet. I cursed, kicked the suitcase and picked it up, and got off the bus once and for all.

I walked over to the streetlight and angrily leafed through Aiby's diary, looking for a clue.

I recalled the riddle she'd left me: *The trials to get there are three. Discouraged you mustn't be. Only a true hero will pass and be free.*

"Dang it, Aiby!" I shouted, thumbing through the diary. "What does that mean? What trials? What does it all mean?"

I shoved the diary into my pocket and inspected the streetlight. It was old and made of black iron with floral designs on it. Swarms of insects spiraled around the light in humming clouds. The two roads ahead looked exactly the same.

Which way? I wondered.

I grumbled and chose a path. After walking about thirty feet, I found myself swallowed by darkness. The road wound into thick forest. I heard creaking branches and the call of an old owl. Not a single star shined in the empty sky.

It makes no sense to keep going this way without even a clue, I thought. *I need to be able to see better. I need . . .*

"Who knows what I need?" I said to myself.

I walked back to the streetlight, examined it carefully, and then sat down on the suitcase. I pulled out Aiby's diary and read it for the umpteenth time in search of even the slightest hint. *If there are three trials to overcome, why not write them down plain as day for me?* I wondered. *What else do I have with me?*

Patches watched me hopefully. *I have the sword,* I thought. *But that's not exactly useful unless I want to go into that creepy forest, which I don't. At all.*

The Night Spectacles will help with walking in the dark, I thought. *But what about the Transmogrifier? I could think of an animal and . . . do what exactly?*

I opened the suitcase.

"You're such a bully, I must say! Hot and wooly, locked away!" Angelica shrieked. I closed the suitcase and sat on it. I couldn't deal with that maniac right then.

95

Thump. Thump. Thump!

Angelica flailed away inside the suitcase for quite some time. A few well-delivered blows made me jump, but I kept my weight on the suitcase until the blows grew weaker and weaker and finally ceased.

A gentle breeze stirred the trees. Patches dashed between my legs and stepped onto one of the two pathways. He growled in the direction of the forest, thought about it a moment, and then barked angrily. Satisfied with himself, he swaggered over to me as if to collect a reward.

"Well, boy?" I asked him. "What now?"

As I patted my friend, I looked up to see a figure approaching.

"Hey!" I called out to attract his attention. He was headed straight for the streetlight.

He was bald and short — he barely came up to my belly button. He wore blue overalls and a checkered shirt. His soft and rosy skin made him look somewhat like a piglet. His hands were clasped behind his back, and he dragged his feet while he walked. When he saw me, he put on a pair of round glasses and eyed me curiously. I let him examine me without saying a single word.

"Bizarre, truly bizarre," the stranger concluded at

the end of his examination. He put away his glasses without adding anything else.

"I suppose you're in charge of this crossroads?" I asked.

"Sorry to disappoint you, my boy," he said. "But I'm just Mr. Tommy."

"Very well, Mr. Tommy," I replied. "Can you tell me where we are and which direction I should take to get to . . . where I need to go?"

Mr. Tommy gave it a lot of thought. He quickly snatched a moth buzzing around his head, studied it with the same curious expression he had studied me with, and then released it.

"Where you need to go depends greatly on where you *want* to go, my boy," he said. "But it just so happens that it's not that easy. And it's not easy because this riddle is a trial. Actually, it's a full-blown literary topos."

I raised an eyebrow and said nothing.

"Do you know what a topos is?" he asked.

"Nope," I said flatly.

He shrugged. "Doesn't matter," he said. The little man hooked his thumbs on the straps of his overalls. "It so happens that one of these roads leads to Right Village and the other to Wrong Village. Now it's well known that everyone who lives in Right Village likes to say things as they really are, while all those who live in Wrong Village do exactly the opposite."

"And which of those two villages did you come from?" I asked.

"Right Village, of course," Tommy responded.

I examined him closely. "Which is true if it's true, but it's false if . . . it's false?"

"Impeccable reasoning, my boy," he said. "Truly impeccable. But returning to your original question, to go where you want to go, it's very likely that you should first go to Right Village. Otherwise you'll never get anywhere."

I scratched my head thoughtfully. Perhaps this all made sense to him, but it certainly didn't to me. "Does the name Sunken Castle mean anything to you?" I asked.

"Yes, absolutely," he replied.

Which could also mean "no" if he's from Wrong Village, I realized.

"And could you tell me which way it is?" I asked.

"I already told you! Head to Right Village and sooner or later you'll get there," he said.

"Which means what exactly?" I asked.

"That at this intersection you must take the right road," the little man replied smugly.

I hate riddles, I thought. *But at least this time a stone giant wasn't going to stomp on me if I got the answer wrong.*

"Just listen, Mr. Tommy," I begged him. "The truth is that I came here to save some friends who are prisoners in the castle and —"

"Yes, yes, I've heard it all before," the man huffed. "It's always the same story. Your good friends have been kidnapped by the evil beings. And surely one of your friends is a maiden."

"A maiden?" I said. "You mean . . . a girl?"

Tommy nodded. His eyes narrowed mischievously. "And she's usually very beautiful," he added.

"It's like you're psychic, Mr. Tommy," I said.

He held up a finger. "Not at all! It's just that heroes have never been known for rescuing maidens with big pimples on their noses or receding hair lines," he pronounced. "Just as heroes never know exactly what to do when they first get in trouble. Overcoming a trial is a vital part of the hero's journey, you see."

"The hero's journey?" I asked.

"That's what you're doing right now, my boy," he said. "Allow me to enlighten you about the details of this classic tale. For one, I'm practically positive that until a short while ago, you were a very angry boy. And when they asked you to go on your journey, you didn't want to know about it. Clearly, you would've rather stayed home."

"Exactly," I said.

"But you went anyway, because you had to," he said. "And you have to go because you're a hero."

"You lost me there," I admitted. "I'm no hero."

"Don't be modest," he said. "Just look back on your past. Something phenomenal had to happen . . ."

"Actually, I just took a weird bus here," I said.

"And now you're here, at a crossroads, and you don't know which road to choose," he said.

Before I could respond, Mr. Tommy added with a know-it-all air, "In order to make the right choice, you have only two possibilities, just as there are two paths at this intersection."

"I guess," I said.

"The first possibility is to avail yourself of a magical object, like those that you probably have brought with you in that suitcase," Mr. Tommy said.

"I see what you're trying to say!" I interrupted. "To take me to the castle, you want one of my magical objects in exchange!" I knelt and opened the suitcase, grabbed the screaming Angelica puppet, and handed her to him.

Angelica flailed in my grip. "Pig! Swine! Ogre! Not fine!" she screamed.

"She's a much better gift than she seems at first, I assure you!" I said.

"Save your hero gear, my boy, and let me finish," he said, wiping his sweaty head. "The second possibility you have for overcoming this difficulty is to rely on a coadjutor."

I flung Angelica back into the suitcase. "A what?" I asked.

"A coadjutor," he repeated. "The word's a bit difficult, like *topos*, but we scholars like difficult words. If anything, the more difficult a word is to say, the more our fingers itch to write it. Have your fingers ever felt that itch?"

"You could say I'm feeling an itch right now . . ." I muttered. *An itch to unsheathe my sword and point it at you until you tell me where that cursed castle is,* I thought.

"A coadjutor is a magical person often borrowed from another story," Mr. Tommy said. "The coadjutor helps the hero overcome a trial and continue in his endeavor. He's a character of fundamental importance to maintaining balance in the story. The coadjutor is at least as important as the hero himself — but sometimes even more so. Quite often, the coadjutor is also much

101

more sympathetic than the hero, despite the fact that it's a difficult role to maintain in the few pages that are generally available for secondary and tertiary characters."

"Do you hear something, Mr. Tommy?" I interrupted, hoping to distract him. I had a hunch he'd go on talking all night if I let him. "I think something's out there. Maybe you could take me to your home where it's safe and explain everything to me better?"

Mr. Tommy's eyes went wide. He stared at me with an expression between admiration and terror.

"Is everything okay?" I asked.

He grabbed my hand and whispered to me in a surprisingly soft voice, "Then that means you're the third type of hero . . ."

"Excuse me?" I asked.

"You need neither a magical object nor a coadjutor," he said. "You can do everything yourself — instinctively." Mr. Tommy let go of my hand and turned around. "Come with me, boy, and I'll take you to Right Village."

I shrugged. Patches and I followed him. Mr. Tommy had led us halfway through the woods when I realized I'd accidentally overcome the first trial. By asking Mr. Tommy to take me to his home, I had solved the puzzle: if Mr. Tommy was an inhabitant of Right Village, he would take me there. And if he were an inhabitant of

Wrong Village, he would have taken me to Right Village anyway since he was obligated to do the opposite.

I think I got lucky, I admitted to myself.

Eventually we reached Right Village. Everyone still seemed to be asleep, but Mr. Tommy didn't hesitate. He escorted me to a building with a sign on it that read:

LAST-STOP STABLES

WE PUSH HARD

TO ALL DESTINATIONS

OR NONE

He put on his little glasses one last time and held out his hand. "It's been a pleasure," he said to me. "In all my years of study, I've never met a hero of the third type."

"Me neither," I replied, returning his handshake vigorously. Since he didn't seem to want to leave yet, I added, "And it was a real honor to meet a coadjutor like you."

A magnificent smile spread across Mr. Tommy's round face. "Remember me if you find yourself in trouble again," he whispered to me. Then he disappeared among the little houses in the village.

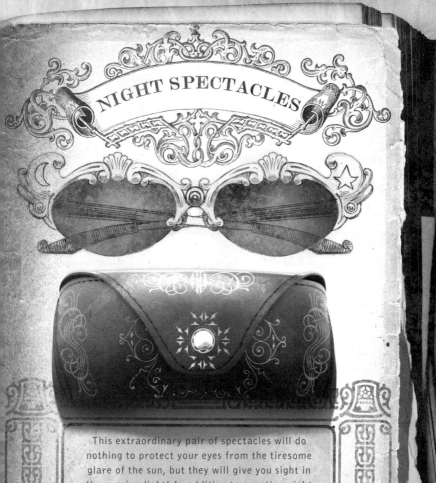

NIGHT SPECTACLES

This extraordinary pair of spectacles will do nothing to protect your eyes from the tiresome glare of the sun, but they will give you sight in the evening light! In addition to granting night vision, these lenses will also prevent wrinkles from forming around your eyes as a result of squinting to see things in the intermittent light. They also look just like regular glasses, so no one will be able to tell you're wearing Night Spectacles.

ENCHANTED 🜊 EMPORIUM

Chapter
TWELVE

JIM,
HORSES, &
MORE RIDDLES

Not knowing what to expect, I knocked on the door to the stables. A deep voice invited me to come in.

Upon entering, I saw nothing and no one inside. Patches moved forward a few steps ahead, intrigued by the scent of manure. At least Patches was still predictable.

As soon as my eyes adjusted to the dark, I saw two horse stalls ahead. As I approached, various horse-related smells flooded my nostrils. A TV showing a black-and-white movie droned in the background. In front of the TV was a ratty old mattress. Atop it was an obese man with a triple chin. His beady eyes stared at me.

"So you're the hero?" he asked as soon as I saw him.

"That's what Mr. Tommy says," I replied, gesturing vaguely beyond the stable door. It closed with a thud.

The man cleared his throat and spat into a copper pot. It tinkled disgustingly. "My brother never understood any of these things. He reads, reads, reads . . . and doesn't do anything else. Life is about much more than reading, don't you think?"

I nodded uncertainly. "Sure?"

"Life's not that, and neither is death," the big man said. "They're both something in the middle, I say."

I didn't reveal that I disagreed. "In any case," I said, "I don't know if you can help me, but I'm trying to get to a place called the Sunken Castle."

The big man shook himself. The mattress springs groaned as if they'd been condemned to die. "Everyone's trying to get to the Sunken Castle at this point, little fella," he said. "But it's not so easy."

"So I've heard," I grumbled. One of the horses in the stalls whinnied, making me shrink back. I saw the nervous steam of its breath billowing in the dark. "But I can assure you, I'm ready for anything."

I opened the suitcase. Immediately Angelica began to shriek. "What smells so old? The horror — it's mold!"

I thrust the doll toward the big man. "Do you want this screaming puppet?" I asked. "It's yours, if you tell me where the Sunken Castle is."

The man stared at me with a blank expression on his face. I shoved Angelica back into the suitcase. With a confidence and voice that didn't seem like mine, I tried again. "How about a pair of Night Spectacles? Or a Transmogri-thingie-what's-it? I'll give you either of the two so long as you don't give me a puzzle to solve, ask me to overcome a trial, give me riddles, or task me with recovering eighteen pieces of a special object that have been scattered everywhere. And since we're talking about deeds, listen up: I don't bring dragons back to life, I don't want to save the world, and I'm not an orphan. I'm not even an only son! No one has made an incomprehensible prophecy about me, so I certainly cannot be a hero. I'm virtually certain I've never been immersed upside-down in a magical pool up to one heel, and I didn't strangle two snakes to death when I was a baby. I don't see ghosts, I don't control the four elements — nor anything else for that matter. I'm a normal Scottish boy who just wants to be asleep in his bed right now, but instead I'm stuck here in this stinky stable — no offense — because I have to rescue my best friend from a meeting that I wasn't invited to in a castle I don't know the location of." I took a deep breath, then exhaled. "With all that said . . . can you tell me where I need to go, or not?"

A considerable silence followed my rant. I felt like I'd exposed this theater of the absurd for what it was, and the man didn't exactly know what role to play anymore.

The man stood, smoothed his grubby undershirt over his big belly, picked up a coachman's outfit from a nearby hook, arranged it haphazardly across his big body, and approached me with a fierce look in his eyes.

Patches heroically retreated to the door while I slipped a hand into the suitcase in the event that I had to draw my sword. Angelica bit my thumb repeatedly while I waited to see what the big man would do.

When we were face to face, the big man cleared his throat, hawked into his spittoon, and said to me, "Now we're talking, little fella. Enough of this tomfoolery." He held out his hand.

I shook it, glad to be done with the charade. His hand was black and greasy like a piston in an old car. "My name's Jim," he said.

"And I'm Finley McPhee — Finley with an 'F,'" I said. "And as I told you, I have to get to the Sunken Castle."

"And I'm here to take you," Jim said.

"Great," I said, hoping he'd let go of my hand soon.

"Usually, in order to be certain about the strength of a person's Voice of Magic, I ask them a question," Jim said. "If they answer correctly, I take them on their journey. If not, I kill them."

"That's . . . a little extreme, don't you think?" I said. Jim said nothing. "No riddles please," I added.

Jim shrugged. "That's how it has to be," Jim said.

"Please no," I begged.

"I have two riddles ready, just for you," Jim said.

"Jim, it's the dead of night," I said. "I'm exhausted and angry and I have no idea what's going to happen."

"Look, I sympathize with your situation," he said. "But we magical creatures are crazy for riddles!"

I sighed. *Definitely crazy, at least,* I thought.

Jim spat a third time. He still hadn't let go of my hand. "So listen up," he said. "I have to kill you —"

"What?!" I interrupted. "You said you were going to ask me a riddle first!"

Jim finally released my hand. "I'm trying to, fella," he said. "'I have to kill you' is the start of the riddle."

"Oh," I said faintly.

"So, yes, I have to kill you, but you can choose how you'll die," he said. He pointed to the first horse stall. "I can take you to a place where you'll be crushed by a five-ton boulder."

"No, thanks," I said.

"Or I can take you to a place where you'll be thrown into a den of lions who haven't eaten in three months."

"I'd prefer the Sunken Castle, actually," I suggested.

"You can be boiled in oil for seven days and seven nights," Jim continued, "or poisoned by the bites of five scorpions, ten tarantulas, and twelve venomous snakes. I can also have you beheaded at the first full moon, or you can be eaten alive by crazed cannibals." Jim dropped his hands to his sides — and waited.

"So what's the riddle?" I asked.

He smiled radiantly. "Which of these deaths would you like me to take you to?" he asked.

Having said that, he turned his back, walked over to the horse stalls, and began fiddling with the lock.

I looked around, perplexed. The stables didn't seem to have any exits besides the horse stalls and the front door I had just come in through.

"Well?" he asked. "Was it a nice riddle?"

I nodded and gulped.

"And don't you want to try to solve it?" Jim asked.

"Not at all," I admitted.

"Oh," he said. "Maybe your dog wants to solve it."

I looked at Patches. "What do you think?" I asked.

He barked twice.

"The second thing you said," I said. "I pick that one."

Jim stopped fiddling and his eyes rolled up and to the left. Apparently he was trying to remember which death was the second one."

"The lions' den?" he asked. "Are you sure?"

"Yes," I lied.

He gave me a huge grin and threw the lock onto the ground, making one of his horses skitter away in fright. "See? I could tell you were a clever one right off the bat!" Jim said. "We just had to do things properly." Jim spat again. "I mean, if the lions haven't eaten in three months, then they're nice and dead, right?" he said. "I mean, nobody can survive for three months without eating!"

I let out a sigh. "So can we go now?" I asked him.

He leaned against the stall. "Don't you want to hear the other riddle?" he asked.

"No way," I said curtly.

Jim shrugged. He pushed open the door, revealing a brand-new motorcycle and sidecar.

"Wow!" I exclaimed. "I thought we'd go by carriage."

Jim tossed me a helmet. "You're a bit behind the times, aren't you?" he said. He sat astride the motorcycle, which sagged under his weight, and turned the key. "What is something that those who make it sell it, those who buy it don't use it, and those who use it fear it?"

I wedged the suitcase between my legs and struggled to get into the sidecar along with Patches. It was like trying to climb into a coffin with another person.

"That's it!" I said, figuring out the riddle. "A coffin."

Jim nodded slowly. "You're a clever customer, Finley McPhee," he said, and we sped into the darkness.

Chapter
THIRTEEN

PATCHES,
PAWS, &
A LATE-NIGHT SWIM

Unsurprisingly, the Sunken Castle really was sunken. In the oppressive dark of that starless night, the castle itself was barely visible. I could just make out the tallest tower and the pitched roof of the keep rising from the black, oblong lake. The water reminded me of the flooded valleys we Scottish people call lochs. I wondered if this lake had a Nessie of its own.

Jim dropped me off and waved to me. "I've never seen anyone get out of here alive!" he said, encouraging me with a pat on the back. Then he zoomed away along the dirt path and disappeared in a cloud of dust.

I took the Night Spectacles out of my suitcase and put them on. My vision improved enough to see the landscape clearly.

Who could have been crazy enough to build a castle in the middle of a lake? I wondered.

I had no idea where I was or how to get inside. Nor did I know why, out of all the places they could've chosen, the shopkeepers picked this place to have their meeting.

I weighed my options. The lake water was ice-cold, so swimming wasn't an option. Neither sound nor light came from the menacing castle. Aiby's diary stated that once the magic shopkeepers had gathered inside, Askell appeared and imprisoned them, but after that part only a few words hadn't been crossed out. All I could read was "The Hall of Mirrors" and something about books in the library.

I heard something move in the water. Thanks to my Night Spectacles, I saw a massive black outline emerge from the water for an instant and then sink back down. Water rippled across the surface.

"I knew it," I muttered, slipping off the glasses. "A lake monster. Is this the infamous third trial?"

I opened the suitcase and took out Lightning Launcher and the Transmogrifier. I could use the sword to fight the monster in the lake, but it wouldn't get me to the castle. What about the Transmogrifier?

Think of an animal and picture it in your head — those

were Aiby's terse instructions, which she apparently thought were perfectly clear.

Think of an animal, I thought. I looked at Patches, then closed my eyes. *Done. Now picture it in my head . . .*

I felt a strange sense of suction. When I opened my eyes, I found myself face-to-face with Patches! The tip of my nose and the base of my tail itched, and I felt like I was cooped up inside my shirt. When I went to straighten it, I discovered that my hand had become a paw! And then I saw something else.

"I have a tail!" I tried to say — but it came out as a series of barks.

Have I become Patches? I wondered. Terrified, I wriggled out of my clothes. Patches — the real one — looked at me with his tongue hanging out of his mouth, acting like nothing weird was going on. I drew back on my paws a bit and noticed that the Transmogrifier had fallen onto the grass next to the Night Spectacles and the sword.

"Now what do I do?" I barked.

I tried to think of a way to reverse the effect, but I couldn't focus due to an irresistible urge to go pee behind a bush. I indulged my newfound animal nature, then continued trying to think. Thankfully only my body had been transformed, because the thought of being trapped in my friend's mind made a chill run down my spine.

Maybe I just need to picture myself as Finley again to go back to normal, I wondered.

I closed my eyes and pictured myself. It didn't work.

I tried again while holding the Transmogrifier between my paws. I pressed it against my furry forehead, but it still didn't work.

It must last for a certain period of time, I thought. But how much? A minute? An hour? A year? I didn't want to think about it.

I trotted to the shore of the lake and tested the water with the tip of my nose. There were some fantastic smells! I put a paw into the water. It didn't seem at all cold to me.

"How do you swim, Patches?" I asked him, barking.

He wagged his tail next to me, completely happy and clearly not understanding what I was saying. *I always have struggled with languages,* I thought.

I looked at the ruins in the middle of the lake and was surprised how poorly dogs saw at night. *That explains why he barks at every noise at night,* I realized.

I thought I glimpsed a faint glow in the sky and wondered what time it was. My stomach growled. Was this how a dog's sense of time worked?

I had no time to speculate. For all knew, it was already too late to save my friend.

Opening the suitcase with the muzzle of a dog was nearly impossible, but luckily Patches helped me.

"Get your paws off me, you ugly animals!" Angelica shrieked. "I'm lovely Angelica, you flea-bitten rascals!"

I really hate that puppet, I thought. Grabbing her in my muzzle, I gnawed on her energetically and then tossed her to Patches. He sniffed at her and batted her on the nose a couple of times. She continued to call us names in barely rhyming sentences.

Finally, we decided to dig a hole and drag her into it.

"Oh no, oh no, what terrible luck!" Angelica cried as dirt began to cover her. "Help me! Help me! I'm buried in muck!"

I had to admit, pushing fresh dirt with my rear paws was a magnificent feeling.

Silence having returned, I dragged my clothes, the Transmogrifier, and the sword into the suitcase, then dragged it to the lakeshore. As I'd hoped, the suitcase floated.

Patches and I placed our front paws on the suitcase and paddled with our rear legs. "Good dog," I barked, unsure which of us I was congratulating.

Paw-stroke after paw-stroke, we gradually made our way toward the ruins of the Sunken Castle.

Angelica

The Sicilian puppetry variation includes thousands of lines of verse that the masters of this theatrical art passed down from generation to generation. The magical marionettes built by Salvo Rosso del Corvo, known as the Playful Puppeteer, have the ability to move and speak their own lines. Over the years, the puppets themselves began to create their own plays. Sadly, the plays have al been lost.

Chapter
FOURTEEN

TRANSFORMATION,
DETERIORATION, &
REFLECTION

I t was a long, long swim. The water was as black as ink, deep, and sinister. I found myself having to stop more than once. While panting and struggling to stay afloat, I felt some invisible force was pulling at me from below. I had to be imagining it, but it felt physical and very real. It made the darkness toy with my mind even more profoundly.

My dog senses were on high alert. I could hear things I'd never heard before, like whistling and various other sounds. The sky itself seemed to murmur constantly, like a lullaby.

We reached the deepest point in the lake. The darkness became total. Clutched by an instinctive fear, I tried to crawl up onto the suitcase, but my little paws couldn't manage it. I saw ripples some three hundred feet away. Something like a backbone was parting the water.

I briefly sank below the water's surface, gripped by panic and struggling to control my new dog body. I turned to look for Patches. Judging by his wide eyes, he'd also seen it. Presumably because he was used to being a dog, he was a much stronger swimmer than I, making it a struggle to keep pace.

The rippling headed right at us, so we swam harder. The suitcase went under for a moment. I saw Patches's head in front of me, his ears aimed at the castle ruins. He looked back to check on me, so I followed his lead.

The rippling in the water was less than thirty feet away from me. I could feel it near me as if it were rubbing my fur the wrong way.

Then it disappeared. The water calmed down. For a few seconds, I didn't notice anything but my panting and the suitcase hinges creaking.

Then I went under.

An immense body swam right behind me in the water. Total darkness was sucking me in.

My brain urged me to swim, but my dog body had other ideas — I froze.

An undertow pulled me down. Slowly I began to sink deeper. The more I sank, the more my panic blossomed.

Something brushed against my tail, making me surge back to the surface for a moment. I gasped in air, but then I began to sink again. I bit into the handle of the suitcase and gripped it tightly between my teeth, refusing to die like a dog.

The water slowly began to go up my nose. The abyss below me seemed to tremble. I swore I heard laughter from beneath me.

The lake creature attached to my tail somehow. It was big — no, enormous! And I was a tiny ball of fur.

I went underwater again, deep into the dark. But I didn't let go of the handle. I held fast with every tooth in my muzzle. And I struggled to hold my breath, to keep my eyes shut.

When my plunge into the darkness finally became unbearable, the undertow was suddenly replaced by an opposing motion. Instead of dragging me in, it began to push me away.

I didn't know why. Maybe I'd passed a test or a trial or whatever. Maybe it was just luck. But I didn't waste any time wondering about it. The thing in the lake had released me and I wasn't going to hesitate.

I surged to the surface, opened my muzzle wide, and swallowed a huge gulp of air. My little paws paddled as hard as they could. I even whirled my tail like a rotor in the hopes that I could catch up to Patches.

"Patches! Where are you?" I barked between breaths.

Bark! I looked to my side. There he was, right next to me! Loyal as a fool — or the perfect friend. My courageous Patches.

A few more long minutes passed. Lake monster or not, we finally reached our destination. We swam through a big window covered with slimy algae. Together we shook out our fur on the floor of the Sunken Castle.

A staircase went down to the floors below. The level we were on sloped unpredictably and was slick with moisture. I sniffed the floor. Sensing no immediate danger, we set forth into the castle halls.

The furniture was dusty and decaying. We passed beneath a large table draped with spiderwebs and crossed a dining room with moth-eaten curtains swaying gently in the night in rhythm with the constant chorus of distant dripping.

We found a large fireplace at the other side of the room. Mysterious echoes came from within. And then, without the slightest warning, the effect of the Transmogrifier ended. My vision improved and became clearer. The wet cold of the night stung my skin. Naked and shivering, I scurried back to the moldy suitcase. I slipped on my jeans, pulled my shirt over my head, and slid my frozen feet into my sneakers.

I grabbed Lightning Launcher and unsheathed the blade from its scabbard to reassure myself. I couldn't help but admire its sharp, shining blade. With Aiby's diary in my pocket, we continued exploring the castle.

We ascended a grand staircase, its steps covered by a worn-out runner, its walls shrouded in white cobwebs. Our steps rang out in the emptiness, echoing down into presumably submerged rooms. Looking down, I saw huge formal tables lazily bobbing in the halls, crystal chandeliers that looked more like pale coral, and floating tapestries spread out like faded water lilies.

I held Lightning Launcher tightly. Its blade projected a faint glow around us that pulsed like a dim beacon. The more I looked around, the more I was gripped by uncomfortable sensations. The castle was a lonely place. Its entire interior gave of a sense of abandonment, a home long forgotten.

Why would they meet in a place like this? I wondered, not for the first time. *And what are they planning to do?*

I reached the top of the staircase, where piles of decrepit picture frames and faded coats of arms lay. We passed through a corridor with vaulted ceilings. The damp had damaged the carpets, and the white wood paneling on the walls was wrinkled like a crumpled-up map. The surviving chandeliers swayed gently in the humid air.

Large canvas paintings on the walls were blackened by mold, rendering the portraits indistinguishable. Countless snails had left a slimy labyrinth of trails on the floor as a sign of their passage.

I pushed on a big, dark door that opened into a hall. As the rusty hinges creaked like the wheels of time, Lightning Launcher emitted a painful surge of light.

"We're here," I whispered.

I had reached the Hall of Mirrors.

The long hall had a large central table with ornamented chairs placed all around it. Two enormous windows on each side gave way to the darkness outside. White curtains made of threadbare gauze fluttered at the sides of the glass panes like immense spiderwebs. Papers and scrolls were strewn on the table and across the floor as if a battle of books had been fought at that very spot.

The walls were the most ominous element of the hall. Made of six huge mirrors, which where angled inward toward the ceiling. A seventh, segmented mirror covered the entire ceiling. An enormous chandelier resembling a golden anchor or a gigantic whaler's harpoon hung in the middle.

My fears grew to irrational proportions. A vague but nearly crippling sense of urgency grasped me.

What is this place? I wondered.

The unnatural and sickly sweet smell of rotten fruit wafted out from the center of the room. As I walked, the scrolls crackled beneath my feet. The floor itself felt fragile and translucent like cuttlefish bones.

I brushed one of the chairs around the table with the tip of my sword. The worn-out wood crumbled to the ground like ashes.

"There's no way," I said to myself. "The meeting of the shopkeeper families couldn't have taken place here."

In the center of the room, where the sensation of vulnerability was strongest, Lightning Launcher's blade began to pulse incredibly fast. Patches froze by my legs.

Slashing the air before me with the tip of the sword, I recalled a line from Aiby's diary. "'And that was when Askell emerged from one of the mirrors,'" I recited from memory.

I looked up and saw my image in the mirror on the ceiling. I stepped forward into the light of the moon to get a better look.

I froze. Shivers ran through my body. The mirror directly in front of me showed Patches standing beneath the legs of a an upright wolf with gray fur. I thought I must still be experiencing the Transmogrifier's effects, because the wolf followed my movements exactly.

He was me.

I watched my reflection stare back at me. *Wolf. Wolf. Wolf,* I thought. *Where have I seen a picture of a wolf?*

I glanced at the mirror to my side and saw a medieval knight with his back to me. Like me, he held a sword in one hand. In the other was a long fishing pole.

"Doug's fishing pole," I whispered, recognizing the item I'd stolen from my brother.

I backed away from the images and bumped into a chair. It crumbled to the floor and I braced myself against the table.

What's in the other mirrors? I wondered.

In the first one I saw a man with my own nose, a long beard, and a tunic from ancient Rome. At his side, instead of Patches, was a donkey with golden fur.

The next mirror showed a nineteenth-century man with long, bushy hair, a pointed beard, and a velvet-trimmed jacket. Instead of a sword, he held a long shining goose-quill pen.

I broke into a cold sweat. *Who are all these strangers?* I wondered. *And why do they look so much like me?*

Slowly I found the courage to move along the table. The chairs broke into pieces as I passed. The mirror on the ceiling kept showing my real image, the Finley I knew, with Patches at his side and Lightning Launcher in his hand. But in the next mirror . . .

I saw a little girl staring back at me. The blood in my veins froze. I had to force myself not to scream. The little girl was holding the same sword in her hand as I was. Patches stood next to her. She looked an awful lot like me. But in some strange way . . . she also looked like Aiby. The way she would've looked as a kid.

"Oh, no," I whispered. I stepped closer. "Aiby?" I whispered. To my horror, the little girl did the same.

Even she was me. It was me in all the mirrors.

"But, but this doesn't — I don't understand," I stammered. I couldn't be them. Those mirrors were liars. They were tricking me. They were mirror thieves!

Or perhaps they're prisoners, I thought.

I turned around. "Doug could be the fishing knight," I reasoned aloud. "Aiby could be the little girl. A nineteenth-century writer would be a fair representation of Mr. Lily . . ."

But what about the wolf? I wondered.

Each of the mirrors enticed me. I could feel their cold surface upon my skin as if I were touching them. Each reflection lured me, tugged at me. But the strongest pull led me toward the last mirror.

So I stared at it. It was a man. He stared back at me.

Inside that mirror was Semueld Askell.

I was him. He was me.

Chapter FIFTEEN

ME,
HIM, &
US

Askell was wearing the same shirt, jeans, and sneakers I was. He was carrying the same sword in his hand. But while my Lightning Launcher was sharp and shiny, Askell's was chipped and emitted a mournful glow.

I raised it over my head, and he did the same. I brought a hand to my face and tilted my head. He did too. Semueld Askell's reflection was missing a large part of his left ear.

"You're not me!" I shouted at the mirror. Askell's mouth mimed the same words.

And the little girl, the old Roman, the writer dressed in black, the knight, and the wolf shouted along with him.

I held the sword over my head. "These aren't mirrors!" I cried.

All seven figures held their swords, pole, and quill aloft. Patches barked. Six dogs and one donkey barked back.

I pointed the sword toward Askell's mirror. "Go away!" I threatened him. "Get lost! I don't ever want to see you again!" When he did the same, I grew furious.

I didn't understand what those mirrors and reflections truly were. Anyway, I was too frightened and too enraged to care.

I shouted, "I am Finley McPhee — with an 'F!'" Then I ran toward the mirror with my sword aimed at my enemy's heart. My image ran at me in the same way, Askell's face reflecting the rage in my own.

Lightning Launcher emitted a blinding flash.

"GET AWAY FROM HERE!" I shouted.

As I struck the mirror, the sword plunged into the glass and passed right through Askell. The blade vibrated in my hand and a web of cracks radiated outward from Askell. Light wrapped around me like a circular lightning bolt. I crashed through the mirror.

I dropped to the ground with my hands covering my head to protect myself from the rain of shards.

But nothing happened. The mirror hadn't shattered.

I had passed right through it.

I found myself in a little room with a gray floor. The only sound was a trickling noise. A stream of crystal-clear water flowed through a crack in the wall and slid into a channel. The stream passed around a sapling with dark berries on its branches, then fell into a well in the precise center of the floor.

I stood up, stunned. The room was small, maybe nine feet by nine feet. Besides that tiny fountain, the well, and the tree with berries, nothing else was there.

But I wasn't alone. I heard someone breathing softly behind me. I didn't turn around.

"Welcome, Finley."

Where is my sword? I wondered. *Where is the Hall of Mirrors?*

"Where am I?" I asked, staring stubbornly at the trickle of water as it vanished into the well.

"You're in the deepest and darkest of prisons, Finley. You're inside your own head."

Then, very slowly, I turned around. Semueld Askell was there in front of me, sitting on a cot.

The prison had no door — in its place was a mirror just like the one I had passed through in the Hall of Mirrors. Now I was on the other side.

But it wasn't a mirror any longer. I could see through

131

it into the hall. The tip of my sword was stuck in the glass. I saw the table cluttered with papers. Patches was running around like a madman, trying to find me.

"I went through the looking glass," I said to myself.

Askell chuckled. "It took me a good deal of time and effort to get you here," he murmured, stroking his damaged ear menacingly.

I said nothing.

"What did you encounter before reaching the Sunken Castle?" he asked. "Dragons? Skeletons? Monsters?"

I clenched my fists. "The three little pigs," I said.

Askell's eyes went wide for a moment, but his cool, angry demeanor soon returned. "Tim, Tom, and Jim," he said. "But you didn't encounter the wolf?"

I said nothing.

"You still haven't figured it out?" he said.

"Figured what out?" I snarled.

Askell smirked. "That the wolf is you."

Rage seethed inside me and I tried to attack him. Askell stretched out his hand and pushed it into my chest, stopping me in my tracks.

His hooked nose was like the beak of a vulture. And on his feet were a pair of horrible metal shoes inlaid with silver and gold. One look and you could tell the shoes were made magical in an age long, long ago.

"You shouldn't be here," I hissed at him. "You were a pillar of salt. You were taken away by the Others. Your people."

"They're not my people, Finley," he said. "I'm not one of the Others. I'm someone like you. Actually, I'm more like you than anyone else in the world. This world — and the other one."

I clenched my fists even tighter. "We delivered you to Oberon and Arthur," I said. "The Others came to take you home and punish you for murdering one of them. I saw them take you away in their fleet across the sea."

"Then let's just say that they changed their minds later on," Askell said.

"Who freed you?" I demanded.

Askell smiled. "I have good friends, you see," he said. "And now, here I am in the last place you would have thought to find me. Inside your head."

I shook my head. Askell laughed even louder.

"Yes, we're really there," he said. "To get here, you had to tear a ticket for the Incognito Bus and take a trip."

I remembered that my name had been written as the bus's destination.

Askell noticed my confusion. "Say it isn't so!" he chided. "You — the great Borderpassing Finley who strides across two worlds — didn't even realize you're asleep! And in your ignorance, you've allowed me to join you in your own most intimate place: your Sunken Castle!"

I shook my head again. I couldn't believe it. It was a trick. It had to be. "Where are Aiby and her father?" I asked. "And where is Doug? And all the others who were supposed to be at the meeting?"

"Oh, Finley, Finley," he said. "We took care of them well before your arrival. You needn't worry about it, believe me. Each of them is like a closed chapter in a nearly finished book. And I'll be writing the final chapter soon enough."

"They're behind the other mirrors, aren't they?" I asked.

"No. Only you and I are in this castle," Askell said. "I've been waiting for you. Only you."

"But why?" I asked. "And for what?"

"When are you going to stop being so mad at me, Finley McPhee?" he said. "It took all my skill to get you to come here. I had to convince you to leave Applecross, get on the Incognito Bus, and fall asleep — all to get you to the precise place where I was waiting for you."

The cot creaked as Askell shifted to reach inside his pocket. He produced Aiby's diary from the same pocket where I kept her diary, in the same jeans. "I had to rearrange various journal entries, remove some pages, and cross out all the words I didn't want you to read. But it was worth the effort, because here you are!"

He tossed the diary at my feet as proof of his act. I bent down slowly while keeping my eyes on Askell and picked it up.

"Diaries are a useful item for leaving directions for travelers, don't you think?" Askell said. "What did I write again? Wait, let me recall: 'The trials to get there are three. Discouraged you mustn't be. Only a true hero will pass and be free.' Not bad, eh?"

I grimaced. "Coward."

"Don't be silly," Askell said. "All I did was write it. It was you who decided to interpret its meaning the way you wanted to upon reading it. Just as all the others did."

"The others?" I said. "Meb?"

"Yes, her, too," Askell said.

I knew Askell was getting at something, but I wasn't certain what. Then again, I understood almost nothing about anything that was happening to me.

"Don't you understand?" Askell asked.

I said nothing.

"You're a tough nut to crack, Finley," Askell said. "In this way, we're very much alike — the two of us, I mean."

"That's not true," I said.

"Yes, it is," Askell said flatly. "You saw it yourself. In the mirror."

"I saw you in the mirror," I argued. "And other strangers who are probably trapped in other rooms like this one."

"The mirrors simply showed you yourself, Finley," Askell said. "All seven of the people you are."

"I'm not seven people!" I shouted.

Askell frowned. "All of us are," he said. "All of us hear voices in our head. You've never heard a voice? Someone who's you, but who's not *really* you, who talks to you and gives you advice? Oh, I refuse to believe it's never happened to you. It happens to everyone. We all have those voices. The Voice of Magic, the Voice of Time, Friends, Places, Fortune, Those Who Are Gone . . ."

While he spoke, I pictured the drawers in Aiby's Secretary desk. I began to fear that Askell was right.

". . . And then, of course, we have our Voice of Darkness," Askell said excitedly. "Something awful. The voice that we want to keep quiet. Closed off, hidden deep down in a Sunken Castle of our own creation where no one else can ever reach it." Semueld Askell rose to his feet and faced me. "And your Voice of Darkness, Finley McPhee . . . is me."

It was too much. I held my head between my hands and squeezed it as hard as I could.

Too much information.

Too many lies. Too many mysteries.

I couldn't trust any of it. No one. Nothing.

I squeezed my head until it throbbed with pain. I lowered my hands and slowly met my adversary's eyes.

"Nothing to say, young McPhee?" he asked me.

"Just one thing," I said through clenched teeth.

I would've liked to tell him that I didn't believe him and that whatever this place was he'd brought me to, I would escape. I wanted to say it mattered little whether it was in my head or in the Hollow World or at the top of the tallest mountain on Earth. I would have liked to tell him that even if I couldn't rescue Aiby, she would rescue me, because she and I were indivisible and nothing could ever separate us. And that even if I, or Aiby, or her father, or Meb, or Doug couldn't save me, then Patches would. I wanted to say that even if all else failed, and I was doomed to die, I would make sure that it'd be the end of him as well. The end of Semueld Askell.

But I didn't believe that. Not any of it. So I only had one thing to tell him.

"If you truly are my Voice of Darkness, do you know what that means, Semueld?" I said to him.

"That you chose the wrong side," Semueld replied. "The Enchanted Emporium will be destroyed. And once it's gone —"

This time, I was the one who laughed.

"Then you haven't figured it out?" I said, shaking with fear and anger.

Askell narrowed his eyes at me. "What?" he spat.

"That if you're my Voice of Darkness," I hissed at him, "then that means I'm yours. And I'm ready to fight you."

Askell flinched. It was nearly imperceptible, but he definitely flinched. And that meant I was right: Askell had a reason to be afraid of me, just like I had a reason to fear him.

This time, our battle would have nothing to do with the keys to the shop. There would be no secret Ark to locate, no Others to keep under control. Nor did it have anything to do with anyone else on either side of the fight.

It was just us. Me and him.

Man to man.

I watched his expression turn from fear to irritation, then to rage, then to a mask of indifference. "You surprise me, Finley," he said. "Unfortunately that's not how it works."

"No?" I asked, still smiling.

"No. The way it works is that now you've come here, and there's no way you can get out," Askell said. He pointed at the well. "Not through there." He pointed at the mirror. "Nor through there. It's a Mirror Prison: one comes in, one goes out. And the person who leaves will certainly not be you."

Without looking away from me, Askell leaned his back against the mirror and slowly began to pass through it.

"You've got water here," Askell said. "The berries from that tree are bitter, but they will sustain you. You'll be bored to death, but you won't die. Give me a smile, Finley McPhee, and in twenty years maybe I'll bring you a book to read."

I charged at him, but it was no use. Askell had passed all the way through the mirror, which closed around him like a pool of water. Once he was on the other side, he shook the hilt of Lightning Launcher, which was still stuck in the glass, bowed mockingly, and walked away.

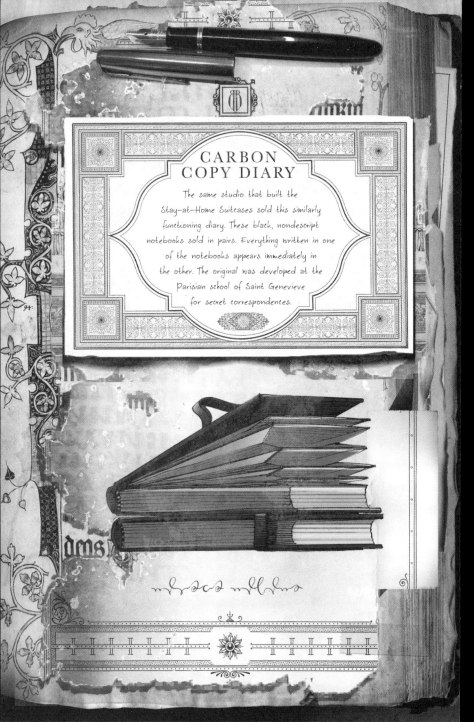

CARBON COPY DIARY

The same studio that built the
Stay-at-Home Suitcases sold this similarly
functioning diary. These black, nondescript
notebooks sold in pairs. Everything written in one
of the notebooks appears immediately in
the other. The original was developed at the
Parisian school of Saint Genevieve
for secret correspondences.

Chapter
SIXTEEN

SOLITUDE,
HEAD GAMES, &
THINKING SMALL

I sat down on the cot. There I was, all alone — with only my thoughts to keep me company.

I'd been cheated every which way. I hadn't saved Aiby, her father, or Doug. And now I knew even less about all of them than I did before this doomed quest had even begun.

Nothing I'd read in Aiby's Carbon Copy Diary was what she'd written. None of them had ever been here. Or perhaps they'd never left.

The Hall of Mirrors.

One enters. One leaves.

I stared at my image in the mirror and refused to blink even when my eyes began to water.

"Patches! Patches!" I cried. "Go get help, boy!"

He couldn't hear me, but that didn't stop me from calling his name until my voice grew hoarse.

I felt like I was losing my mind. I examined the cell inch by inch in search of some sort of clue.

I tried to accept the things I saw. I tried to believe that this little room was really a prison. If that were true, then there'd be at least six other cells around me, linked together by one mirror on the ceiling in the Hall of Mirrors. Even though it all seemed so utterly complicated, I kept thinking, kept trying to reason everything out inside my head. While I was inside my own head. I thought about the seven voices, the seven drawers, and the seven mirrors. My mind reeled.

I shoved my hands in my pockets. To my surprise, I found the Transmogrifier in one. *It must have slipped into my pocket when my jeans were in the suitcase!* I realized.

Trembling with fear and faint hope, I got up from the cot. I was already imagining myself transformed into something that could go down into that well and . . .

I peered down the well's sides. Nothing but darkness.

I stretched out my arms and felt the sides. They were smooth and damp.

Maybe a bird could make it, I thought. *I could transform into a bird and fly down.*

No, I thought. *A bat. Birds can't see in the dark, but bats can. With echolocation, maybe I could find a way to flee this prison.*

My heart beat wildly as a multitude of panicked thoughts assailed me.

How long will the transformation last?

How long did I remain Patches?

What will happen to me if the effect of the Transmogrifier ends when I am in a tiny pipe, underground, or who knows where?

I closed my eyes and tried to focus.

"One comes in, one goes out," I said, repeating Askell's words.

To leave the cell, someone else has to enter it, I realized. But who?

Askell again?

The wolf?

The little girl?

The man with the quill pen?

The knight with the fishing pole?

Someone else entirely?

I had never felt so alone.

I gripped the Transmogrifier and thought.

And thought some more.

I refused to let myself despair.

Then I burst into tears. I cried buckets.

Everything had just become too much. It was too big for me.

Time passed. I didn't know how much. I had no way to tell.

I drank from the well and ate a couple of berries. At least Askell had been telling the truth about the berries. They were the most bitter-tasting thing I'd ever had to swallow.

I banged on the translucent surface of the mirror and called for Patches again. I wondered why the light was always the same, day or night, both inside my prison and outside.

"Do you hear me?" I screamed at the other mirrors.

Nothing.

More time passed. And I thought.

Eventually I decided that I, Finley McPhee, was the Voice of Time. That meant my Voice of Magic had to be the wolf — the one who scared the three little pigs. That very fairy tale was the one my grandmother had always told me to get me to fall asleep when I was younger. And there was a picture of a wolf in Aiby's drawer, along with the swimsuit and the key.

So all of it was true.

The voices, Finley, I thought. *Focus on the voices. Keep figuring out who you are.*

"The knight with the fishing pole," I thought aloud.

I loved to go fishing. Before Aiby arrived, it was my favorite thing. I'd even been held back at school because I'd gone fishing for seventy-one straight days instead of attending school. It was something I was ashamed of, so perhaps that's why my image was facing away from me.

No, I decided. *I'm happy when I'm fishing. Sure, I feel bad about skipping school now, but at the time I felt completely at peace in my secret place down by the water.*

That meant the knight was the Voice of Places.

"The old man and the donkey has to be my Voice of Those Who Are Gone," I said. "I don't know why Patches would be a golden donkey, but nothing else makes sense for that one."

And Askell is my Voice of Darkness, I thought. Even though I knew it was true, I couldn't bring myself say it. But I accepted it.

Two of them remained: the Voice of Friends and the Voice of Fate. One had to be the nineteenth century gentleman with the quill. The other had to be the little girl. While she looked a little like Aiby, I didn't feel at all like we were friends.

"The little girl must be Fate," I decided.

I wondered how the old guy could be a friend. It felt like guessing . . .

I smiled. It was all wrong. It made no sense.

I couldn't believe anything Askell had told me. His frightened face gave that fact away when he realized that I knew I was his Voice of Darkness just like he was mine.

And then there was what Mr. Tommy had told me. "He said I'm the third type of hero," I murmured. "The one who doesn't need magical objects or a coadjutor. The one who can do everything by himself."

I had to get myself out of that prison. I had to figure out where I was. I had to get myself back home. And then I would find out where the others were. I'd find out why Askell had said they were closed chapters in a nearly finished book.

I had to rescue them. If it was still possible, that is. If they still needed rescuing.

"They knew about it," I muttered. "The Lilys knew they would get caught. That's why they prepared my suitcase. And left me Angelica. That's why they didn't invite me to the meeting. And why they didn't invite Meb."

Meb was still there at the Enchanted Emporium. Waiting. At least she was safe. That comforted me.

It was a small comfort, but a comfort nonetheless.

Small and insignificant, just like that little ant that was walking across the floor of the cell by my feet.

"Wait a second!" I said. "How did you get in here?"

I dove to the ground to examine it more closely. There was no doubt about it. It really was an ant.

One comes in, I thought. *One goes out.*

Where had this ant come in? From under the mirror? From the well? Maybe from the crack in the wall that the water was dripping from?

I swallowed hard. Becoming an ant was much better than becoming a bat and flying down a well that probably didn't have an exit.

On hands and knees, I followed the ant all around the room without ever losing sight of it. I examined every square inch of the cell in search of a crack, a passage, or some slight opening.

And then I found it: a tiny crack in the wall near the base of the mirror.

"I'm sorry, but you can't leave now," I told the ant. Ever so gently, I lifted the ant from the floor and carried it to the other side of the well. With that done, I grabbed the Transmogrifier and pressed it to my forehead.

TRANSMOGRIFIER

The **TRANSMOGRIFIER OF SIR CHAMELEON** lets the user assume the form of any animal the user knows well enough to imagine in its entirety. The physical transformation does not affect the transformed user's ability to think, but instead grants him the instincts and sensations of his chosen animal.

Chapter
SEVENTEEN

TINY,
NAKED, &
ALONE

It's incredible how long it takes an ant to get out of a pair of jeans. Every fold becomes a mountain. It's kind of like steering a boat in the middle of the ocean. But I did it.

In case you've never experienced what it's like to be an ant, let me explain: you feel the air vibrate around you like some sort of enticing music and a pleasant scent combined. And if you follow that resonant scent, you generally get where you want to go.

During my experience as an ant, I can remember thinking about only two things: food and home.

The scent of home came from the wall, near the tiny chink next to the mirror that I'd found. I slipped inside and crawled on my little feet through a dark, microscopic maze, guided only by that indefinable tug

toward "home." As I skittered along, I tried very hard not to imagine what would happen if the transformation was reversed while I was still inside such a small space.

Shortly after, I emerged from the wall and cowered, dazed by the infinite possibilities I had for moving around. Yet I couldn't stay still. As it turns out, ants never stand still.

I kept following the aroma coming from home. It felt like the most satisfying thing in the world, the only thing that mattered. I scurried along, trusting my instincts and ignoring everything else.

And then, when I least expected it, I found myself sitting on the floor in the middle of the Hall of Mirrors, completely naked and happy as a clam.

I recovered instantly, possibly because of how cold the floor was against my butt. I stopped to look at Askell's mirror, which Lightning Launcher was still stuck inside. The mirror was covered with cracks, but I could still recognize Askell's features.

The fact that my clothes were still inside that cell made his appearance even more disturbing. Nude Semueld Askell was the last thing I ever wanted to see.

"One comes in, one goes out," I repeated to the mirror. "Stay strong, little ant. Sooner or later I'll find a way to set you free."

Then I grasped the hilt of Lightning Launcher and tried to yank it out of the mirror. It was deeply wedged into the wood frame behind the mirror.

I pulled harder. The muscles around my neck bulged tugged on the sword with all my weight and might.

"I . . . WON'T . . . LEAVE . . . YOU . . . HERE!" I cried between tugs.

The sword moved a little, then a bit more. When it finally came free, I found myself holding the sword with the cold floor once again chilling my butt.

I breathed a sigh of relief, stood, then cut off a piece of curtain and draped it around my shoulders like a toga. I'm not sure of it, but I think the ancient Roman reflection nodded ever so slightly in approval as I passed.

I left the Hall of Mirrors, dragging the sword behind me so it would make as much noise as possible in resolute defiance of Askell's evil plot.

When I was in the middle of the staircase, I heard a noise coming from below.

Is it Askell? I wondered, shivering. *Or maybe the wolf?*

I raised Lightning Launcher, determined to fight whatever stood in my path — no matter how terrifying it was. Then Patches poked his head out from behind a piece of furniture.

"Patches!" I cried. And he ran to me.

We hugged each other. I barely felt the icy floor beneath my feet.

"I know, I know," I kept repeating, whining into my dog's ear. "I missed you, too. But you could have come looking for me, you know."

Meanwhile I listened and watched for any signs of movement, but there was no trace of Askell. It seemed as though only Patches and I remained in the castle submerged in that dark lake — and our images in those strange mirrors.

I reached the half-submerged window through which we'd originally entered the castle. Patches whined softly. "What is it, Patches?" I asked.

Like some kind of responsible border collie, Patches persuaded me to follow him into a huge room where a neglected fireplace had blackened an entire wall. He disappeared behind a broken chest and fumbled around, trying to pull out something heavy that was hidden behind it: my Stay-at-Home Suitcase.

"You're amazing, Patches!" I told him, and this time it was completely true.

That suitcase meant I could change clothes — but only if I could let Meb know she needed to put some into the corresponding suitcase back at the Emporium.

I opened it. Inside was the tiny mirror with the silver

frame that I'd found on the beach . . . and a book. I blinked in surprise. Its title was:

Through the Looking Glass and What Alice Found There

It was a beautiful edition of the book written by Lewis Carroll, with gold leaf inlays and a dark red cover. It showed two kids behind prison bars, trapped inside a book, which looked awfully familiar — and terrifying.

I felt the tingling of magic beneath my fingers. *Why did Meb send me this book?* I wondered. *And how did she know I just passed through a mirror?*

I grabbed the silver mirror I'd found on the beach and finally took a close look at myself in the reflection.

I was me. Just me.

I set the book on the ground and calmed myself by petting Patches.

It really was a strange book. It clearly belonged to the Enchanted Emporium. I didn't open it. My instinct, or maybe it was a voice inside me, told me to leave it be.

And so I did.

I was no expert on books. Beyond reading the title on the cover and noting the illustration, I didn't know what else to do with it.

And then, for some reason, I thought of my coadjutor.

Chapter
EIGHTEEN

AN OLD BOOK,
THE SUBCONSCIOUS, &
DIGGING

M r. Tommy? Mr. Tommy?" I yelled through the streets of Right Village. Or rather, I wheezed. I'd had to run along all the dirt roads that I had traveled earlier in the sidecar, and I was exhausted — but determined.

"Mr. Tommy!" I shouted again.

I didn't know which house was his, so I tried every single one of them. But the windows were barred and the lights were off. It seemed to me there wasn't a living soul in Right Village. Besides, it was still nighttime inside my head.

"Come on, Patches! Bark!" I ordered my dog.

We split up. After a bunch of attempts, a revolting orange door finally opened partway. Through the shaft of light that seeped out, I recognized Mr. Tommy's face.

He wore a blue nightcap, and he was carrying the stub of a candle in a copper candlestick.

"Who's that calling my name?" he said. As soon as he recognized me, he exclaimed, "Ah, it's you!"

"Mr. Tommy! Do I ever need you!" I said.

Before he had time to say something weird, I handed him the book I found in my suitcase.

"What do you make of this?" I asked. Then I added, "I recommend you don't open it. I've got a feeling it might be dangerous."

"Oh, I find that hard to believe, my boy," Mr. Tommy muttered. "It's just a book. But please, come into my home — though I must warn you it's a bit untidy."

I followed him into a cottage crammed with piles of books, all of them face down and open. I recognized a couple that I'd once begun but didn't finish. I don't know why, but that thought made me feel a little guilty.

"Come in, come in, sit down," Mr. Tommy said. "Can I get you up a cup of tea?"

"No tea, Mr. Tommy!" I cried. There's no time for tea! I need you to look at this book and tell me all you can."

"Really?" he protested. "What's all this rush about?"

"It's your moment," I whispered to him. "Your moment to become a real . . . what's that word again?"

156

He put on his spectacles and gave me a long, studied look. "Coadjutor," he said. He looked at the book. "Seems to me it's a very unusual edition of *Through the Looking Glass and What Alice Found There* by Lewis Carroll."

How clever of you, I thought, barely able to stop myself from saying it out loud.

"Which is also the pseudonym of Charles Lutwidge Dodgson, a writer and first-class mathematician, as well as a lot of other," Mr. Tommy said. He brought out a lens from who knows where and began to gradually pass it over the whole cover. "It's the second book of Alice's adventures, and I would say it's quite the curious edition as I have no idea who the boy depicted on the cover with Alice could be."

It's me, I thought, but I remained silent.

"I know that the first edition is from 1871, but this copy seems to be even older," Mr. Tommy proclaimed. "Almost ancient, actually. Why don't we take a look at the book's publication date." He began to open the front cover.

"Don't open it, please!" I begged him.

"Hmm," Mr. Tommy said. "My boy, if I can't open it, it will be extremely difficult for me to tell you more about it. I mean, you can't quite judge a book by its cover, now can you?" He squinted and stared at the spine of the book. "Hmm. There is something odd here on the binding where the name of the publisher is . . ."

"What is it?" I asked.

He showed me an elegant silver logo that looked like the stylized silhouette of an octopus. "'Octobooks Publishing' is written here in silver. If I tilt it this way, it's as if it's printed over something else that's much older. It's a strange stamp of some kind, I'd say." He put down the book. "In any case, I've never heard of Octobooks Publishing before."

I hadn't either. "Is that all?" I asked.

"I'm afraid so," Mr. Tommy admitted.

I began walking around the room nervously. "Do you have a pen and some paper, Mr. Tommy?" I asked.

"Of course," he replied, passing them to me. In the meantime, he continued to study the book.

I figured I'd try my old method of solving mysteries. I wrote:

List of the few things I know for certain:

1. Aiby and her father went to a meeting with Doug. They should come back Sunday afternoon, but Meb and I (and the seagulls) are convinced that something bad happened to them.

2. Askell had Aiby's travel journal with him. When I asked him what happened to Aiby and her father and Doug, Askell replied that they were a "closed chapter."

158

3. I found a book in my suitcase that just felt wrong — my instincts told me not to open it. The publisher is unknown. It seems to have been made especially for me.

I stayed still for a while, pen in hand, before adding:

4. Aiby and her father knew they were in danger, which is why they didn't take me or Meb to the meeting. Aiby wrote that I should ask Angelica for help and prepared the Stay-at-Home Suitcases for me.

5. I buried Angelica for the second time next to the lake. Maybe that wasn't such a good idea.

6. Only Meb could have put that book in my suitcase, which means it has to be for me.

I examined the cover with the bars and the prison as well as the silver octopus on the spine.

7. I found a silver pocket mirror on the beach.

"Mr. Tommy?" I asked. "Does silver mean anything to you?"

"It's a white precious metal that —"

"No, Mr. Tommy," I interrupted. "I meant to ask about silver's magical properties."

"Oh!" Mr. Tommy said. "It's a nocturnal, lunar metal associated with the unconscious and emotions. It's also used to protect travelers, especially ones at sea."

"Maybe . . ." I said. An idea had popped into my head. Even if it didn't pan out, I had nothing to lose.

I grabbed the silver pocket mirror from the suitcase. "Protect me now," I murmured.

"Can you tell me what you intend to do?" Mr. Tommy asked.

"Just trust me," I said. "And close your eyes!"

I opened the book without reading the pages and held it up to the mirror. I saw the swirling and flickering letters of Incantevole but made sure I didn't read any of them.

I slammed the book shut. "Now I understand why Askell said that Aiby and the others are a closed chapter," I said. I rubbed my chin. "You know something, Mr. Tommy? Evil people talk too much. They just can't resist the temptation of letting everyone know how great they are and doing so reveal their evil plans."

"That doesn't surprise me, my boy," Mr. Tommy said. "Typically, in traditional stories, the villain explains everything at the end because —"

I cut him off. We didn't have time for a lecture. "We don't have any time to lose, Mr. Tommy," I said. "And I still need you — and your two brothers."

"To do what?" he asked.

"To get away from here with me," I said. "As soon as possible."

Mr. Tommy slipped on his overalls and checkered

shirt and went to wake up Mr. Jim and then Mr. Timmy. Soon after, Mr. Jim took me back to the lake in his sidecar. There I dug up Angelica, who bombarded me with insults the entire trip back.

Angelica's insults pleased Mr. Jim. "If only there were women in our world with her temperament!" he said after we'd returned to the village. "Today's women are so namby-pamby."

Soon we'd reached the crossroads. In the square next to the streetlight, Mr. Tommy started arguing with Mr. Timmy to convince him to get the bus going again and take me back.

"I can't, Tommy!" Mr. Timmy said. The Incognito Bus's stubborn driver kept rearranging the baseball cap on his head and seemed decidedly worked up. "I just can't do it and you know it! Ours is always a one-way trip. You can't change the way things work!"

Jim turned off the sidecar engine. "What was I telling you, Finley?" he said. "My brother reads too much. And the other one watches too much TV."

I ignored them. I motioned for Patches to get on the red bus while I tossed the suitcase inside. I had Lightning Launcher firmly attached to my belt. The feeling of its scabbard bumping into my leg gave me a sense of confidence and security I'd never felt before.

The three brothers continued to bicker amongst themselves. I couldn't tell what even one of them was actually saying.

"QUIET!" I shouted. They stopped speaking. Mr. Timmy arranged his baseball cap nervously, Mr. Tommy shook his head and adjusted his round spectacles, and Mr. Jim spat out a glob of phlegm. Patches stared at me through the windshield. All eyes were on me.

I pointed at the red bus. "Mr. Timmy, I need you to turn on the engine for me."

Mr. Timmy blew his nose. "That's easily done," he said. "But I cannot drive it. Will you do it yourself?"

I rested my hand on the hilt of the sword. "Of course," I said.

Mr. Timmy took off his hat, put it back on, and then took it off again. "In that case, maybe the regulations would allow it," he said. "But then again, there's —"

Mr. Tommy's gesture cut Mr. Timmy off. "Oh, drop it, Tim," he said. "Regulations are just guidelines."

Mr. Jim nodded. "Agreed!" he crowed. "Just give him the dang keys already. Finley's one of us, after all."

Mr. Timmy took a few moments to consult the regulations, then reluctantly agreed to the plan. To be safe, he slipped the key into the ignition and told me how to adjust the driver's seat.

"A well-placed seat," he explained, "is the secret of safe driving. And treat her well, okay?" he added, patting the steering wheel.

"You can count on me, Mr. Timmy," I said. But when I heard the bus engine chug to life, took stock of the steering wheel's enormous size, and evaluated the countless controls and buttons on the dashboard, I asked him, "Could you turn it — err, *her* — in the right direction for me first?"

So that's how I found myself driving an enormous red bus along the twisty, bumpy road of my subconscious back to Applecross. Or at least, that's how I pictured the long return trip would go.

It should go without saying that I knew how to drive a little bit. Dad had taught me to move the van, and I'd done so many times. But there is a big difference between parking a van in your front yard and maneuvering a double-decker bus along a treacherous mountain road.

The entire ride seemed uphill, too, as if I was coming back from a place that was at the bottom of the deepest, darkest, best-hidden valley in all of Scotland. And if you think about it, that's not too far from the truth.

The road went on and on for I don't know how many miles. At the first junction I reached, I turned on the high beams so that I could read the only sign:

The Road to Applecross
Not recommended for beginning drivers.
No large vehicles or trailers allowed after the first half mile.
At least I knew I was on the right road.

The bus climbed through the hairpin turns while the mirrors hanging from the windows swayed like attendees at a concert. Patches whined after each curve as he got tossed repeatedly from one side to the other. Even the suitcase banged around while Angelica ranted like a preacher proclaiming the apocalypse was nigh.

I still wasn't sure why I'd retrieved that aggravating doll. But that was only one of many things that I was unclear about:

The strange, enticing book. The mirrors. The prisons.

They were all connected. They had to be.

That moment, the headlights of my monstrous bus lit up a dam I recognized well. Despite feeling exhausted, seeing the dam reinvigorated me. "We're coming, Aiby," I said. "For all of you."

I felt even better when I passed over the mountaintop and saw the breathtaking view of Applecross Bay below.

Just then, a faint gleam brightened the sky behind me. I'd returned almost exactly at dawn. The sea below stretched out like a silk blanket between the dark cones of the islands of Skyle, Robha Chuaig, and Rona.

I stepped on the gas and somehow managed to speed through the first hairpin turn. Going down turned out to be much harder than going up. Every time I touched the brake pedal, the juggernaut screeched to a halt, forcing me to accelerate immediately to prevent the bus from stalling. It was a war filled with hiccups, rumbling, and the clinking of mirrors underlined by cursing and frantic barking.

Somehow we managed to get to the bottom of the mountain safe and sound. The agony of the Incognito Bus's final trip continued until the first houses in town, where we popped out of that final curve like a pellet from a slingshot.

I breathed a sigh of relief. At that very moment, the brakes gave out.

"Haaaang on!" I screamed, swerving wildly.

The bus tilted sideways, causing two wheels to lift off the ground. It teetered for a brief moment before it fell on its left side with a thunderous crunch. We squealed along the asphalt for over a hundred feet before grinding to a halt in a mountain of smoke.

Patches, Angelica, the suitcase, and I wound up squashed against the windows, sore but otherwise unharmed.

"Everyone okay?" I asked, taking off my seatbelt.

Patches wagged his tail from under the seat where he'd ended up, seemingly wanting to do it again. Meanwhile, Angelica railed insults at me while dangling from the rearview mirror.

I crawled out of the driver's compartment, recovered the suitcase, and stuffed its contents back inside. Since the bus door wouldn't open anymore, I used the sword to break a window so we could climb out.

After pulling Patches free from the wreckage, I breathed deeply while taking in all of Applecross. As the salty sea air filled my lungs, I jumped to the ground with the suitcase in one hand and Patches in the other.

No one seemed to have noticed the crash. Surely, townsfolk as hungry for gossip as Applecross's citizens would come running at the sight of a double-decker bus grounded on the beach. Something was amiss.

As I examined the town, I realized that all the houses facing the beach had their shutters closed. No one was at the pub, either. And I didn't see a single person in the streets or at the rectory.

Patches and I walked to town. Outside the church, I called out for Reverend Prospero but received no reply. When neither Mr. Everett nor the McStays appeared at their front doors after I'd knocked, panic took hold of me.

"Help! Help!" Angelica shouted. For once, she and I were thinking the same thing.

Applecross seemed deserted. *Have they disappeared?* I wondered. *Maybe everyone is still asleep?*

Whatever the real answer was, I knew Askell was responsible.

"Meb! Meb!" I called from outside her design shop. I wasn't expecting an answer, so when I didn't get one, I pushed open the door.

"Meb?" I murmured.

I entered and listened. The refrigerator droned. The faucet dripped. I unsheathed my sword and crept forward as stealthily as I could.

"Meb?" I repeated.

I reached the dripping faucet in the kitchen and turned it off. Everything was in its right place — except for the fact that Meb was gone

I grabbed a pair of pants and a clean shirt for myself and slipped on a pair of shoes that were just a tiny bit too big for me. But they didn't smell like wet dog and mold, so it was a welcome change.

I found the mate to my Stay-at-Home Suitcase sitting on the sofa. Next to it was a stack of recently opened mail. As I approached the letters, Lightning Launcher's blade lit up with a faint glow.

I leafed through it. Some letters, bills, a copy of the *London Book Review*, and some wrapping paper from a recently opened package. *The Old Library of Skyle Island* was written beneath the sender's postage stamp.

Strange, I thought. As far as I knew, there was no library on Skyle. The closest thing we had to a library was Mr. Everett's meager (boring) collection of books. Every once in a while a van visited the school or stopped in the meadow where the campers were, but we had no traditional library anywhere.

"Jules!" I cried out at that point, startling poor Patches. I'd seen our busy postman delivering books to several people just the day before. *What could that flurry of book deliveries mean?* I wondered.

And there had been a note in Aiby's diary about books from a library. Had she meant the library on Skyle Island?

"But there's no library on Skyle," I repeated to myself.

Angelica flew into a rage. "Oh, isn't this funny!" she cried. "There is a library, you dumb bunny! And it's there that they did go! All who dared read were tricked by the foe!"

I stared wide-eyed at that obnoxious puppet. When I finally spoke, I did so through clenched teeth. "Help me understand, Angelica," I growled. "Are you telling me that you've known all along that the meeting of the families was going on at a library on Skyle Island?"

"Of course I knew that!" she crowed. "Everyone does, you dingbat!"

I was so angry I almost couldn't speak. "Why. Didn't. You. Tell. Me. That. Right. Away?" I roared.

"Because you didn't ask, you creep! Besides, twice now you've buried me deep!"

"Paaaatches!" I shouted, running out of Meb's house. "Start digging a hole! And make it deeper this time!"

INCOGNITO BUS

Belongs to the group of public transportation
vehicles for visiting the collective unconscious.
These magical objects were originally of Arabic
design before they were taken as spoils of war by
Charles Martel after the Battle of Poitiers. Soon
after, they were adapted to various geographical
contexts: a yellow, American taxi, a moped in
Barcelona, and even a bicycle in Amsterdam.
The valiant Orlando rode an Incognito rocket
to visit the moon in a famous song.

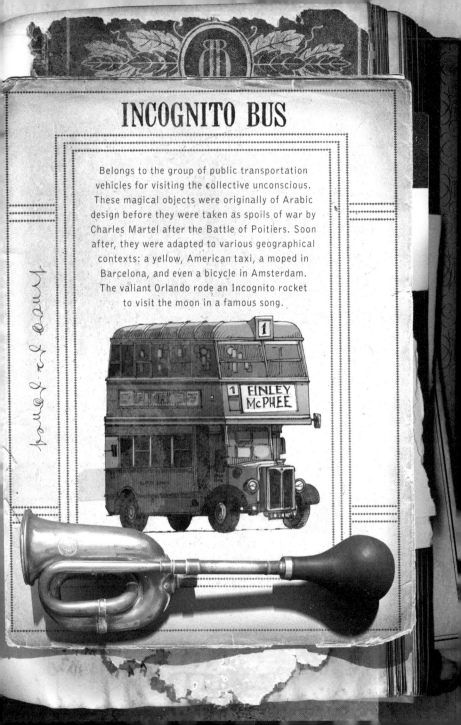

Chapter
NINETEEN

INTERROGATION, INFILTRATION, & EAVESDROPPING

My interrogation of Angelica about the location of the Old Library lasted for nearly half an hour, but all I got in response were rhymed insults. Only after I held her face to face with Patches and threatened to bury her for a third time did that devil-doll spill the details.

Angelica may have been a children's toy, but I swear that puppet was pure evil. In any case, she told me exactly where on Skyle the library was located.

"Well, Patches," I said. "We're gonna need a boat."

Lucky for me, my brother Doug was sometimes as predictable as Patches — he always had his motorboat fueled up and ready to go at the dock in front of the Greenlock Pub. When we got there, I untied the boat from the dock, launched it into the sea, hopped on board, started the engine, and zoomed away.

Together Patches and I watched Skyle Island draw near. "Here we come!" I said to my trusty friend.

We reached the shore as the sun began to peak above the mountains. The mountaintops were cast in golden-brown splendor. I pulled Doug's favorite sunglasses out of the boat's glove compartment. With his shades on my face and my sword at my waist, I beached the boat on the island's shore like a movie star.

I cast a long shadow on the beach — and I felt every bit as tall, confident that I would save my friends.

Patches and I climbed up a nearby trail until we reached the main road. From there, we followed a twisting path along the shrubs. Even though it was early morning, there were other people around on Skyle. I heard the engine of a distant car, the honk of a horn, and other normal signs of life — not at all like Applecross had been, which gave me some comfort.

According to Angelica's instructions, I needed to climb up to an old cottage that was surrounded by trees.

With my dwindling strength, I climbed in the direction she had indicated. Luckily I found it on my first try. The cottage was surrounded by a thick privacy hedge and thorny bushes. Beyond it was a small garden.

The building was made of brick and had white window frames and a blue door. Five windows long and three high, it boasted an array of chimneys on the roof. And, oddly, Jules's postal van was parked in the front.

Curious, I thought. *What was Jules doing here?*

I approached the entrance by skulking along the hedges. As I drew closer, I noticed a freshly polished brass plate next to the blue door that read: *Old Library.*

I tiptoed past the shrubs until I reached one of the corners of the building. Without any difficulty, I skirted along the shortest side, making sure to duck beneath the first window. At the second window, I peered inside and saw a typical Scottish living room: wall-to-wall carpet on the floor, wood paneling on the walls, and standard wooden furniture. Nothing more.

I continued to the large porch in the back. A glass and wood structure sat in the center of a large, beautiful garden. Some benches were scattered among the hedges. A black gazebo and a wooden kiosk were in the distance. Behind them, a little gate led to the countryside.

The most surprising element was the hot-air balloon belonging to the Tiago family. It was secured to the branches of a cherry tree with a few iron anchors. I recognized it because I'd seen it the day the Enchanted Emporium had opened.

"We're in the right place," I said.

We stayed hidden among the shrubs, hoping to see

someone walk onto the porch. After a long while, no one appeared. So I gathered my courage and crept to the door that led onto the porch. Luckily, it was unlocked.

"Stay here, Patches," I whispered.

I snuck into the house. The porch had two large wicker couches with white seats. Newspapers, several of which weren't in English, were strewn across the cushions. The delicate scent of a wisteria plant filled the room. As soon as I set foot on the wood floor, it creaked. I froze. The melody of violins came from the house. It gave me the creeps, though I couldn't say why.

I risked a couple more steps only to make the floor squeak again. I slipped behind the couches and slowly moved for cover behind a large vase.

My ears perked up as I heard voices. Male voices. I held my breath and scurried from the porch to the doorway leading to the house. My path to the door was around fifteen feet long with no cover, but I had no other route to take.

After a quick dash I found myself walking across soft, silent, wall-to-wall carpet in a narrow hallway with nowhere to hide. The voices had grown louder and I could pick up a few words now. I passed under some Chinese lanterns.

At the end of the narrow hallway, I found myself in

the foyer — in front of the blue door I'd seen from the outside.

Three doors were open. The center door led to the stairs, and I decided against that route right away as I'd had enough of squeaky wooden floors for one day. The voices were coming from the door on the right. Without thinking too much about it, I chose the door on the left. When inside, I crouched down behind some containers overflowing with books. I realized I was in a grand library. It had mauve walls, a big, round mirror, a computer atop an old desk, and heavy curtains drawn across the windows. If someone came in, the only other hiding place was behind a Chinese-style screen.

Partly relieved but still frightened, I was finally able to listen to the conversation taking place in the room opposite from my hiding place. I was certain I recognized the voices speaking: one was that of Professor Edwin Everett, the owner of a gift shop in Applecross. He'd been behaving strangely ever since the Lilys had come to town. I still wasn't sure if he had something to hide or not, since teachers tend to be a bit eccentric even in the best of times. I'd also previously eavesdropped on his conversations and they were always hard to follow.

That day, Professor Everett's conversation was crystal clear — especially when I heard Semueld Askell respond.

Chapter
TWENTY

EVERETT,
ASKELL, &
IMAGAMI

"Luckily, it's Sunday, and Jules didn't make a fuss when I asked for the van," Professor Everett said.

Askell grunted in response.

"During your morning run, I took a final drive around the houses," the professor continued. "And I recovered the last dozen or so of the books."

"All read?" Askell asked.

"Yes, all of them had been read," the professor answered.

I heard glasses clink together. "To our prisons!" the professor said.

"Don't celebrate too soon, Everett," Askell warned. "Not yet."

"Then when?" Everett asked.

"Soon, very soon," Askell said soothingly, as though speaking to a child. "After we hear from the Queen of the Others and confirm that everything went as we expected. Indeed, everything has gone better than even our most optimistic predictions, don't you think?"

"According to my list, we have almost three hundred books that have been read," Mr. Everett stated. "That is to say, we were able to ensnare about half of the town, including everyone we were interested in: the McStays, McBlacks, and the two McPhees."

My breath caught in my throat. *What happened to my parents?* I wondered.

Askell snickered. "I'd call that a success, then, Professor Everett," he said. "And they say people don't read anymore. If you want someone to crack open a book, all you have to do is send them a free one!"

"Provided it's the right book for the right person," Everett added.

"Oh, of course," Askell said, laughing. "The Golden Bough for that wild Legba was a brilliant choice."

"Whereas the last Ulysses Moore book was a great match for the young Moogleys," Mr. Everett said. He seemed to be reading from a list of book assignments. "Shakespeare's *Tempest* for Prospero was wise, too."

"Especially fitting in that particular case, Mr.

Everett," Askell said. "My compliments. Without your advice I would never have managed to trap them all inside those books."

That's what his plan is! I realized. *Good thing I trusted my instincts and didn't open that book. The shimmering Incantevole words that I saw in the mirror would've captured me just like the rest.*

Just how many have they caught? I wondered.

To my horror, I realized that the boxes I was hiding behind were filled with many volumes bearing the Octobooks seal on their spines. Each book was unique and likely meant to grab the interest of a specific person. It was the perfect trap for any reader.

"You should have seen them, Everett," Askell continued. "The expressions on their faces when I turned up at the meeting. If you'd seen the Lilys' reactions — especially Locan! And that dunce, Doug, who wouldn't stop staring at my ear. We were lucky he was there instead of his brother."

"Oh?" the professor said. "Why is that?"

"Finley is suspicious," Askell said. "With him around, it would've been much more difficult to make the other guests believe the books were gifts from the Lilys."

"But you got rid of him for good, right?" the professor asked.

"Correct," Askell said. "There isn't a more complicated prison in existence. Whoever tries to escape it goes insane. I give you my word as an Askell, which, as you know, is as good as —"

"False," Professor Everett interrupted.

"Watch what you say, Everett," Askell growled. "Our partnership isn't over yet. Not until we enter the Enchanted Emporium, find and restore the Ark of the Passages, and return it to its rightful owner!"

"Is she here yet?" Everett asked.

"Not yet," Askell said. "But she won't be much longer now." Askell glanced around at the books in the library. "Where are the books with the Lilys and their companions trapped inside?"

"They're here," Everett said, presumably pointing at some nearby books. "One, two, and three. The last one was delivered early this morning."

Meb, I realized.

I heard the sound of several books being tossed aside. "I say let's start with this one," Askell said.

"It's your plan," the professor said. "I'm just a —"

A sudden buzzing noise interrupted their conversation.

"She's here," Askell said, standing. "Get ready!"

They hustled out of their room and headed straight

toward me. I dove behind the screen a moment before I would've been discovered. Askell stepped into the library, produced his Cloak of Mirrors from a drawer, and set it on the desk next to a laptop.

I flattened myself between the screen and the wall, trying to keep from breathing too loudly — and hoping he couldn't hear the furious beating of my heart.

The buzzing grew stronger, filling the air with the sound of thousands of tiny, furious wings.

"They're here!" Askell boomed. He took a white computer cable in his hand and pressed it against — and into! — the mirror on the wall. The reflection in the mirror dissipated, then formed itself into the shape of a face. As the image in the mirror came into focus, I saw a woman's face. She had dark skin and almond-shaped eyes. Her pupils seemed to change color depending on what she said — or maybe what she thought. I recalled the glasses with the multicolored lenses I'd seen Aiby use . . .

"Hello, Askell," said the woman in the mirror.

Askell bowed to return her greeting. "My queen, I'm very pleased to see you," he said, his voice dripping with regality. "Today's the great day, finally, when we enter the Enchanted Emporium."

"We're going in?" she asked.

"Everett and I will," Askell said. "And with the Lilys' blessing."

"And how can you be sure they'll let you go in this time?" she asked.

"Because I'll make them," Askell said.

"How?" she asked.

"I've got the books from Abdul Alhazred's Burning Library with me," Askell said. "And I made them read them."

"You used the library of that crazy firebrand?" she asked. "And what did you have to promise him in exchange for their use?"

"That's an agreement between him and me, Imagami," Askell said. "You needn't worry about it."

"And Locan Lily didn't notice the books were from the Burning Library?" she asked.

"Oh, no, he couldn't have recognized them," Askell said. "You see, I altered the books with a silver stamp and a new name: Octobooks."

The woman smiled. "Quite original, I must admit," she said.

Askell beamed. "They're all in those boxes now," he said. "They're ready to come with us and assist with the destruction of the Enchanted Emporium. Our plan is simple: First I'll read a few pages from this." Askell showed the woman a book. Then he slipped it into a paper bag. "That will free one of the guardians of the Emporium. And when I free them, I'll ask them for the keys to the Emporium."

"And if the guardian you release refuses to give them to you?" she asked.

Askell snickered. "I'll start burning the other books before their eyes," he said. "Or maybe I'll tear out the pages, one by one."

"Evil has a new name: Askell," the woman said.

Semueld bowed his head, clearly satisfied. "Today I will give you back what was stolen from you," he stated.

"Rein in your pride, Askell," she warned. "You've said the same thing before and failed. Your Voice of Darkness is strong . . ."

Askell sneered. "Finley can't interfere this time," he said. "Besides, he's just a child."

"Once again, I've heard these claims from you before," she said. "But you know by now that the two of you are mirror images of each other, which is cause for concern — and fear."

Askell snapped something between his hands. The fragments of a crushed computer mouse crumbled to the floor.

"Anger makes you blind, young Askell," she said.

"And it makes you underestimate your adversaries. You've used two magical objects from the deepest abyss: Abdul's Library and the Sunken Castle. Those who look too deeply into the abyss shall find it staring back at them . . . or into them."

"It's time to shatter the mirrors, Imagami," Askell said through clenched teeth. "And it's time for us to make our move. Now."

Neither person spoke for a long moment. I held my breath.

"Go ahead, you impetuous youth," Imagami finally said. "But I warn you: this is the last chance I'm giving you — and that Oberon and Arthur have given me."

"You told me that when you freed me from the salt."

"I freed you because Oberon and the Others allowed me to," she said. "Because even they don't know which side is the true one."

"The Men of Time?" Askell said. He spat. "You can't be serious."

"The Men of Time are obsessed with time, my treacherous Askell," Imagami said. "But the magical creatures are equally obsessed with magic. And just as you don't control time, we don't control magic."

"Not yet," Askell hissed.

"Yes," Imagami murmured. "Not yet. Bring the object back to me and you'll get whatever you want." Her face began to scatter.

"Those are the words I've been waiting to hear from you," Askell said with a snarl. He bowed stiffly and waited until Imagami's face had completely disappeared from the mirror. Then he lifted the laptop above his head and shattered it against the desk.

"Cursed old hag!" he screamed. He grabbed his Cloak of Mirrors and left the room. "Let's go, Everett! It's time!"

He flung open the blue front door, donned his cloak, fastened the buckle, and flew away and into the sky as a murder of crows.

The
NECRON
OMICON,
OR,
The book of the names

Written by the...El Hazzard,
Do...John

...ANTWERPIAE
1574

LIBRARY OF ABDUL ALHAZRED

The writer H.P. Lovecraft provided potential information about this infernal library after claiming to have read one of its evil books, *The Necronomicon*. Every book in the library is cursed, making them particularly dangerous to the uninitiated. The library also includes *The Book of Madness, The Fatal Joke* by M. Pytyon, and the burned books from the library of Alexandria.

OCTOBOOKS PRINT

Chapter
TWENTY-ONE

THE SWAP,
THE DRIVE, &
AN OPEN BOOK

From behind my cover, I watched the crows rise over the bay. I heard Mr. Everett's footsteps in the upper story of the house. Askell had left him the book on the desk — the one in the paper bag.

Mr. Everett was whistling. "Hurry, scurry!" he said to himself.

I moved as quickly as I could. I pulled the book out of the bag and replaced it with *Through the Looking Glass*. I ran out of the library, dashed through the carpeted hallway, took a sharp turn onto the porch, and sprinted outside and into the garden.

When the coast was clear, I whispered, "Patches! Patches! Where are you?"

Without waiting for Patches to appear, I ran toward the postal van to search for the key, but it wasn't there.

I went to check the van's rear door and breathed a deep sigh of relief when it opened. Inside I found the other boxes of Askell's evil books.

Just then, Patches appeared next to me. Without bothering to explain, I tossed him into the van and immediately climbed in behind him. I pulled the door halfway shut from the inside and fumbled around, trying to hide myself behind the books along with my dog. My sword still hung around my waist, and the book I had taken from the bag was clutched to my chest.

"I'll explain everything later, Patches," I said soothingly. "Just please try to keep quiet, okay?" He licked my hand and I knew he'd understood.

A few minutes later, I heard Mr. Everett's steps on the gravel. He approached the van, opened the rear door, and dropped another load of books in front of us. Without noticing us, he closed the door and climbed into the driver's seat. He dropped something on the passenger seat, started the engine, and departed.

Patches and I held each other in the back of the van. The rear had no windows, so we were bathed in complete darkness. The van jolted stiffly over each and every pothole, causing the books from the cursed library to shift from one side to the other. I unsheathed Lightning Launcher and used the light it emitted to examine the book I had taken from Askell. It was *The Old Curiosity Shop* by Charles Dickens. It had a red and black cover, which lent it an elegant and sinister appearance. The cover art portrayed two little boys looking into a storefront filled with old and mysterious objects. I noted miniature toy soldiers, skulls, hourglasses, and dinosaur bones. The back cover featured a figure dressed in black with a cloak falling over his shoulders. I immediately recognized his face: it was the same as the writer I had seen in one of the mirrors in the Sunken Castle.

I wasn't sure what to make of the fact that one of my reflections seemed to be Charles Dickens. I took a deep breath and put my hand on the cover of the book. *Whatever is happening has already been written,* I thought.

While Mr. Everett drove, I thought about what I should do. Since he was whistling calmly, I concluded that he wasn't aware of my presence or the fact that I'd taken the book in the bag and slipped another one inside. I had sensed from looking at the books with my silver pocket mirror that they were designed to trap readers inside, but I had no idea how to get them out. I wasn't sure if each book could imprison multiple readers, either.

But I was confident I could figure everything out. Given the number of books around me, and the ones I had heard Askell and Everett talking about, I figured there was a book for each specific reader. *The Tempest* for Reverend Prospero, for example. The reverend was a huge fan of Shakespeare, so Everett had chosen wisely.

The thought of my father and mother being trapped somewhere in the pages of these books made me want to cry. The fact that one of the guardians of the Emporium was imprisoned in the book I held between my hands made me want to punch somebody.

When I heard the wind whistling below us, I knew that Mr. Everett had reached the bridge connecting Skyle Island with the mainland.

Another broken promise, I thought. I'd vowed to never to cross that bridge again. Instead I wound up riding across it without a say in the matter. Trying to guess your own future truly was senseless — especially when someone else was in the driver's seat.

Soon Everett would take the north fork and ascend to the dam and then descend into Applecross on the same road I'd taken on the Incognito Bus. Then again, he could also continue to the right and travel the rest of the six miles along the coastal road.

I tried to think. Askell told the Queen of the Others he was going to free one of the guardians of the Enchanted Emporium to force them to hand over the keys. To free them, he was going to read a few pages of their book.

That makes sense, I decided. *If they work anything like the Mirror Prison in the Sunken Castle, then after opening the book and reading a few words the person imprisoned inside could be pulled out by a second reader.* I grimaced. *But does that mean the second reader would take the first reader's place inside the prison?* I wondered.

"One comes in, the other goes out," Askell had said in that singsong voice of his. Except this time, no ants would be able to take my place. There would be nothing unexpected this time to facilitate an escape. That unlucky ant that wormed its way into the magical prison of my mind would do me no good in this scenario.

Mr. Everett accelerated the van. I petted Patches and weighed my options. If I opened the book and read it, I might be imprisoned inside, too. Or I would pull Aiby or Mr. Lily out, then together we could search for a way to save the shop — and the others.

"Dear Charles," I whispered to the illustration of Mr. Dickens on the back cover. "I hope you're a Voice of Friends, or only Patches will be left to protect us."

Patches curled up against me, covered the book with his wet nose, and whined softly. "It's okay," I reassured him. "It's a risk worth taking."

I opened the cursed edition of *The Old Curiosity Shop.*

FEAR,
FOLLY, &
FREEDOM

As I flipped past the first page, the letters on the page begin to flicker before my eyes in the incomprehensible Enchanted Language of Incantevole.

I groaned. "Oh, man," I said. "I can't believe this. The text stays in Incantevole even after it captures someone!"

I quickly flipped through the pages hoping for just one page of English, but there was no doubt about it: Abdul's entire library of books were written in Incantevole.

Figures, I thought. I couldn't read the Enchanted Language at all. Aiby had insisted that I learn how, but the letters only stayed fixed in my mind for a fraction of a second, then shortly thereafter became little more than elegant scribbles on a page.

I'm one page away from freeing Aiby, I realized, *and I can't read a single word of it.*

Tears streamed down my cheeks. I felt like an idiot. A donkey. A fool. A goose — and not the golden kind.

"It's impossible!" I cried. I squinted at the letters. A few of them began to wriggle, becoming legible characters. I made out an "L" and an "A," but no more.

No words.

I threw the book at the van's door in frustration and held my face between my hands. "Stupid," I said to myself. "What did you expect, Finley? What language would a cursed book that could trap people inside it be written in besides Incantevole?"

I banged the back of my head against the van. "Did you think it'd be a picture book?" I said, berating myself. "A Magic for Dummies instruction manual?"

Aiby told me once that everyone knew the language of Magic when they were born, but the longer they spent in the world of Time, the more they forgot the language of Magic. She told me they forgot about magic because they were scared . . .

Scared of what? I wondered.

I dug my fingernails into the side of my head. "Stupid," I told myself.

No, Finley, a voice in my head said. *You're not stupid — you're afraid. You've only ever been afraid.*

Afraid of what? I asked.

That it would be easy, said the voice in my head.

I laughed. In a strange way that kind of made sense. Then again, if I was hearing voices in my head again then perhaps I couldn't trust my own mind. I leaned my forehead on the van's metal wall. It was red, just like the red wooden ship, the red bicycle, and the red bus.

What's the deal with all this red stuff? I wondered — or maybe I asked. Either way, I got a response.

Red is the color of the Voice of Darkness, one voice said. *The Voice of Magic is violet. Blue is the color of the Voice of Places. Every voice has its color, just as every magic has its voice. But it wasn't always like this. Before the Magical Revolution, when new magical objects were still being invented, red was the color of the Voice of Friends.*

I was going crazy. That much felt obvious.

It's just because you're afraid, Finley, the voice urged.

"I'm not afraid!" I cried out so loudly that I worried Mr. Everett had heard me. But the van calmly continued along its path. "I went to an unknown land to save my friends! I escaped from the Sunken Castle! I'm not afraid of anything!"

But you are afraid of yourself, Finley, a voice said.

Afraid of myself? I asked.

Afraid of your abilities, the voice said. *Afraid that you can read Incantevole perfectly, but you just don't want to.*

Why wouldn't I want to? I asked. No answer came.

"Doug reads it perfectly," I snapped. "Why isn't he here with me? Why do I always have to do everything? Why do I have to be so . . . so . . ."

Doug wasn't there. Neither were Aiby, my parents, Meb, or Mr. Lily. Horrible things were happening and I was the only one left who could do anything about it.

I was the only one. I was . . . alone. That was the fear.

I shook my head angrily. *Why didn't I go to school for seventy-one days?* I asked myself. *What's so hard about school? And what's so hard about reading Incantevole?*

Nothing. I just had to *want* to do it. To do anything, easy or hard, you had to want it above all else. You couldn't realize your potential if you didn't establish a method, a system, a routine — and concentrate on just one thing at a time.

That's just it, Finley. You have to want it. You have to try. This last thought was not my voice. It belonged to my friend, Mr. Dickens. So I wasn't alone. Plus I still had Patches.

One thing at a time, Finley, I thought.

I moved around the van in a frantic search for the book I'd thrown. I heard the wind blowing to my left, on the side where the sea was, and realized Mr. Everett had chosen to travel along the coastal road.

I used Lightning Launcher to create some light and managed to find *The Old Curiosity Shop*. I flipped it open and knelt in front of it.

I was furious. Furious and focused.

I wiped my stupid tears with the back of my hand and tried to take a deep breath, but I faltered three times. So I kept taking deep breaths until I managed to calm myself down.

"Now it will work," I said to myself. "Now I'll open this book and be able to read it like I've known how to all along. It'll be as if it isn't the hardest thing in the world, but just one hard thing in a long list of many other hard things I will have to do through the course of my life. Because there are things that have to get done. Pretending otherwise just makes them harder." I glanced at my trusty friend. "Right, Patches?"

My dog leaned his muzzle on my leg, and I realized I wouldn't have ever gotten this far without him.

"Although it may be difficult, Patches," I said, opening the book to the first page, "I'll read all of this to you — from start to finish!"

Patches' ears pricked up. I focused on those dancing letters, those cryptic, lingual snakes, those ink blots. I faced them in single combat, one by one.

"I'm reading you," I said. "I'm reading you and understanding you . . ."

But in reality, nothing happened. The letters continued to slip around beneath my gaze, the signs spinning around in my mind like a swarm of wasps.

My eyes burned holes into the book. I blocked out everything else around me. "I'm reading you," I said, louder now.

The dancing characters on the page slowed to a waltz. Little by little, the letters stopped dancing altogether, and they began to pose in peaceful stillness. I read the words aloud.

"Night is generally my time for walking. In the summer I often leave home early in the morning, and roam about fields and lanes all day, or even escape for days or weeks together . . ." A paragraph was etched out, so I continued reading where the text picked up again, "and, if I must add the truth, night is kinder in this respect than day, which too often destroys an air-built castle at the moment of its completion, without the least ceremony or remorse." Another missing section. ". . . is it not a wonder how the dwellers in narrows ways can bear to hear it with Doug!"

And at that point I stopped reading. *Doug?* I wondered. I tried to reread the last word, but it had vanished. The Enchanted Language had vanished before my eyes . . . and the letters had become normal to me. I read aloud again:

". . . constant pacing to and fro, that never-ending restlessness . . ." the page went blank and picked up again farther down with, "is it not a wonder how the dwellers in narrows ways can bear to hear . . ."

"Oh!" a voice I knew very well cried out near me.

"Doug?!" I whispered. "Doug, is that you?"

I saw his profile in the middle of the boxes. Patches jumped on top of him.

"Down, Patches! Quiet!" my brother said.

"Doug — is that really you?" I repeated.

"Finley?" he said. "Finley!"

I tossed the book aside and tackle-hugged my brother. "Doug, you're back!" I cried. "I did it!"

He seemed dazed. "Did what? Where are Miss Nell and her father?" He glanced around with a dumb look on his face. "This isn't Covent Garden in London . . . where are we, Finley?"

I grabbed his head between my hands and squeezed it. "I read Incantevole, Doug!" I cried. "I did it! See, you were imprisoned in this book, *The Old Curiosity Shop*! But I pulled you back out of it, Doug!"

My brother rubbed his head. "Pulled out?" he repeated. "Man, I don't understand anything you're saying, Viper. The last thing I remember is we were at the Old Library on Skyle, and then I found myself transported to London. And now . . ."

I smiled at him. "And now you're in the back of Jules's postal van, in Applecross," I said. Then I bragged, "And this is Lightning Launcher, my new sword."

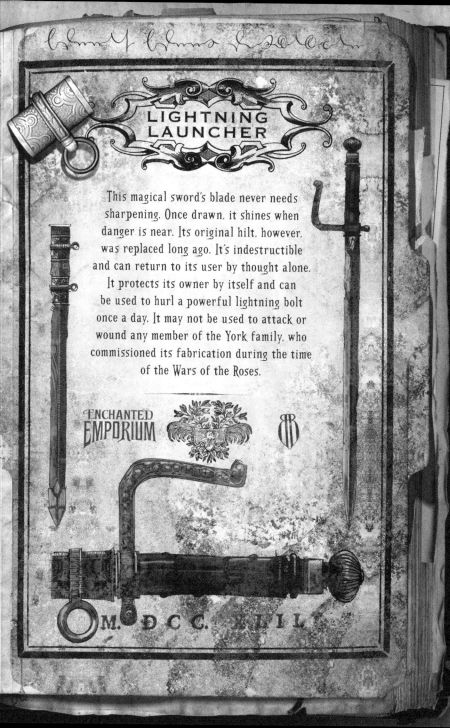

LIGHTNING LAUNCHER

This magical sword's blade never needs
sharpening. Once drawn, it shines when
danger is near. Its original hilt, however,
was replaced long ago. It's indestructible
and can return to its user by thought alone.
It protects its owner by itself and can
be used to hurl a powerful lightning bolt
once a day. It may not be used to attack or
wound any member of the York family, who
commissioned its fabrication during the time
of the Wars of the Roses.

ENCHANTED EMPORIUM

M. DCC. XLII.

Chapter
TWENTY-THREE

ASKELL,
THE PROFESSOR, &
THE EMPORIUM

Before Jules's van reached Reginald Bay, Doug had time to tell me everything that had happened at the meeting of the shopkeeper families. I'd already figured out parts of it thanks to various clues and what Askell had said, but the details Doug shared painted the whole picture for me.

Askell had revealed himself last, descending the staircase theatrically, as if he had been in the Old Library all along. As if the building was his house.

"He climbed down from the roof, like a storm of crows," Doug explained. "Askell tried to talk, but none of the others cared to listen to what he had to say. Instead, they disbanded the meeting right away. The representatives of the various families spread out in the

house and the garden and chatted. It was at that point when the guests began to disappear inside the books, one by one. Askell did this by having them find the books as if they'd discovered little gifts left for them by the Lilys. Since the shopkeepers knew all about the Lily family's fondness for books, no one had been suspicious."

Doug broke off and frowned. "Aiby and Locan were the last two to be caught," Doug said after a moment. "I think they figured out it was a trap and Askell forced them to read their books."

"How did it feel being trapped in a book?" I asked.

He shrugged. "It didn't hurt," he said. "But I kept hearing a constant noise in the background that sounded like distant voices."

"And how were you caught?" I asked.

"I found this book in the bathroom," Doug said. "And you know how it is . . . in certain situations, a book can seem completely irresistible."

I told him about Askell's plan, and Doug admitted he didn't know which books the others were trapped in. But the books were here in front of us. The only reason I held back from opening and reading all of them was that I had no way of knowing which of them had already been read and which were still waiting to trap their first reader instead.

To avoid getting trapped in our own literary prisons, we needed the list Mr. Everett had on the seat next to him. But before we could decide on a plan, the van slowed down. The sound of pebbles under the wheels told me that we'd nearly arrived.

Doug told me to pick a plan, but I wasn't sure what to do. It felt like a desperate situation. I clutched the hilt of my sword and thought.

The van suddenly braked. Mr. Everett jumped out of the driver's seat and cursed. When I figured the professor was far enough away not to hear, I used Lightning Launcher to break the lock from the inside. Doug, Patches, and I slipped out.

It was mid-morning, but someone had lit a large, crackling fire in front of the Emporium. A black column of smoke billowed upward. From behind the van, we saw Professor Everett join Askell by the bonfire.

Askell looked our way for only an instant, then turned his back to us. "Do you know what this means?" he asked Professor Everett.

We moved closer to be able to hear and see better. Four people were lined up in front of the shop, creating a line between Askell and the Emporium. As soon as I saw who they were, my heart caught in my throat.

"It means what I just told you," came Reverend

Prospero's thunderous voice. "You cannot enter, Semueld Askell!"

"This place doesn't belong to you!" added my father, who stood next to the reverend.

A feeling of hope lifted my heart.

"What does this mean, Everett?" Askell thundered a second time.

The professor stammered and gestured vaguely. "I don't know, Semueld! They should not . . . be here."

I grinned. *Yet here they are,* I thought. *Reverend Prospero, stubborn McBlack, and both of my parents!*

Doug pointed at Mom, who held a rifle over her shoulder. "What a woman!" he whispered. I felt an emotion that I still can't quite describe.

"I went by their houses myself to get their books!" the professor said to Askell. "And they were . . . they were right where they belonged, Semueld!"

"I should spit in your face, Everett!" McBlack snarled. "You're a traitor! You're nothing more than a grubby paper pusher! To think about everything we told you, you lily-livered coward!"

Reverend Prospero motioned for him to be silent. Askell drew back and opened his arms in a gesture of goodwill. "Gentlemen," he said. "You don't understand what you're doing. Nor what you or I are capable of."

"Oh, yes we do," my father replied.

"Just go back to your friends, Semueld Askell," Reverend Prospero commanded. "And tell them they can't go through Applecross."

"You've no idea what you're unleashing," Askell said.

"We're not unleashing anything at all, you blackguard," my mother said.

Doug and I looked at each other and grinned. When push came to shove, our mother was every inch as tough as our dad. Maybe tougher.

Semueld Askell gestured wildly in frustration. "Have you ever heard such nonsense?" he cried.

"I suggest you depart, Askell," the reverend said.

"This house is MINE!" Semueld Askell snapped.

Prospero positioned his body so that it filled the entire entrance to the Enchanted Emporium. "This house was built by Reginald Lily for himself and his family over a century ago," said with surprising calmness.

"So what?!" Askell screamed. "The Lilys are a family of THIEVES!"

"Whether that's true or not," the reverend said icily, "is entirely your problem."

Askell tried to compose himself. He pointed at the door. "I need to go in that house!" he whined. He took a deep breath, then growled, "And you can't stop me!"

Askell slipped a hand beneath his Cloak of Mirrors and pulled out a long, rusty sword with a black hilt. "I didn't brave the madness of Abdul's Burning Library, nor plunge into the depths of the abyss to be stopped now! Let me in this house — and I'll let you live!"

Askell twirled the rusty sword twice and pointed it at the foursome lined up in front of the Enchanted Emporium.

Reverend Prospero stepped forward. The soles of his shoes resounded against the ground like the dinging of a bell. "So what do you intend to do?" Prospero said. "Attack an unarmed man?"

Askell bared his teeth. He howled like a beast and lunged with the sword in front of him.

Reverend Prospero didn't move. The sword ripped through his clothes and dug into his side. He opened his eyes wide, pressed his hand to the wound, and crumpled.

My father ran to his side to support him.

"Enough," McBlack growled. He leveled the shotgun at Askell and fired. The echo of the two shots rang between the white stones of the cliff. The seagulls scattered. Two empty cartridges fell to the ground.

Askell lowered his sword. He was unharmed . . . and smiling. His rusty sword flared with dark energy. "You still haven't figured out what you've unleashed," he said.

McBlack reloaded his shotgun. My father and mother pointed theirs at Askell. "Don't take another step forward, you scoundrel!" my mother crowed.

Scoundrel? I thought. *Blackguard? Mom, if we get out of this alive, I'm gonna give you a long lesson on insults.*

I slipped out from behind the van. When Doug looked at me, I said, "Sorry, bro, but I think it's my turn."

"Hey!" Doug cried. "Viper, wait!"

I sprinted toward the scene. My father fired two shots before Askell sliced the smoking barrel of his rifle in two with his sword.

I heard my footsteps ring out on the white stones of the cliff. I felt the black gaze of the seagulls. I heard the mysterious song of the sea.

I heard my mom shout, "Finley, no!" Her voice wrapped around me like a shield — one that no magic sword in the world could cut through.

I had almost reached my adversary. His Cloak of Mirrors reflected my sword at a hundred different angles. I saw my eyes reflected, too. They were yellow and sharp, like those of a solitary predator.

My hand was joined to the hilt of the sword as if it were a claw. I bared my teeth and something deep inside me growled at Askell, "Hey, little boy. The wolf is here!"

RUSTY THUNDER

ENCHANTED
EMPORIUM

The twin blade to Lightning Launcher,
this weapon was commissioned by the Yorks' rival
family, the Lancasters, during the long and bloody
Wars of the Roses. It has powers similar to those of
its twin, including an indestructible design and the
ability to return to its user's hand by thought alone. It
originally allowed its owner to hurl a lightning bolt once
a day, but this power has been lost due to improper
upkeep. Any time it wounds an opponent, it saps the
victim's strength and transfers it to its wielder. It may
not be used to harm any member of the Lancaster line.

Chapter
TWENTY-FOUR

RUST,
LIGHTNING, &
CLAWS

Askell spun around to face me in a cacophony of reflections. And as soon as he saw me, he let out an inhuman scream and lunged at me with his sword.

Zing!

Lightning Launcher directed my hand upward and deflected Askell's blow, sending his black sword twirling to the ground. For a brief moment I felt the sweet taste of victory. But a second later, the sword rematerialized in Askell's hand.

"You can't be here!" Semueld Askell shouted.

"Sorry for the delay," was all I could think to say.

Askell charged at me while twirling his sword like a barbarian and bombarded me with blows. One, two, three — seven lunges and slashes in an increasingly frenzied pace.

I let Lightning Launcher direct my hand as it parried one strike after the other. But Askell's slashes were strong, heavy blows that made my bones and muscles tremble.

I parried, dodged, and then backed up, overwhelmed by the fury of his attack. Askell was twice as big as I was and twice as fast. But no matter how hard he tried, his sword couldn't get past my guard.

And so, after a sequence of slashes that could've killed an army, he took a step back and held the black blade in line with his aquiline nose. I couldn't help but look at his severed ear.

"Who taught you to fight like that?" he said, panting from the relentless attack.

"No one," I said. And it was the truth.

Askell took a deep breath and continued his assault. He lunged and made me step aside, I slashed and he stepped back. We changed places like a whirlwind of metal and flesh. Out of the corner of my eye, I saw McBlack had finished reloading his rifle and was following our every move. He hadn't pulled the trigger because we were too close to each other to fire safely.

Askell broke off his attack and backed up for a moment. I pointed Lightning Launcher's shining tip at him and said between gasps, "Do you give up?"

"Would you?" he snarled.

Then he pulled the hood of his Cloak of Mirrors over his face and disappeared.

I froze. "Coward," I hissed through my teeth. *Where is he?* I wondered. *Where?!*

"Finley!" McBlack called out from behind me.

Lightning Launcher jerked in my hand, twisting my wrist painfully to deflect Askell's blow a moment before it would've dug into my spine. I saw Askell only for the instant that the two blades clashed into each other. Then he disappeared again.

Screaming from the pain in my wrist, I lost my grip on Lightning Launcher. It fell to the ground.

"Return to me!" I ordered it, and it reappeared in my right hand. I passed it to my left hand a moment before Askell attacked me a second time. I leapt backward as the two swords clashed. Once again, he disappeared.

A third blow blocked, then a fourth. They arrived out of nowhere but somehow Lightning Launcher knew where to parry.

I deflected another blow, then started to back away. *Concentrate, Finley,* I told myself. *Don't think about anything else — not the shop, the cliff, the van, or the fire. One thing at a time. Concentrate on fighting. Focus on him. How can you know where he's going to attack from?*

I had a fraction of a second between Askell's blows. And I was holding the sword in the wrong hand. I raised the sword in front of my face and kept backing up until I could no longer feel the waves of heat coming from the bonfire. The fire provided good protection on one side, at least, so I circled to keep it to my right. I dug my feet into the pebbles covering the cliff and prepared for Askell's next attack.

That's it! I realized. *Even if Askell is invisible, his footprints aren't!*

I stopped looking in front of me and lowered my gaze to the ground.

I breathed quickly, trying to get more oxygen to my aching muscles and my burning lungs. My right wrist was turning violet.

Concentrate, Finley, I thought. *The pain doesn't exist.*

I heard the crackling of the fire and the gulls screeching. I sensed my parents, Mr. Everett, and Doug all moving around in my peripheral vision. But I didn't look at them. There was only one thing I had eyes for. Something insignificant and tiny. One of those things that only an ant would notice.

There! I said to myself. A few pebbles were flattening beneath Askell's invisible feet. I realized he was moving slowly to my left where I was most exposed.

I smirked. *I know where you are,* I thought. *And you don't know that I know.*

I hid my smile and turned a little to my right to tempt him to attack my left side. Askell took the bait. As soon as I saw a large patch of pebbles move, I turned and slashed where I knew my adversary would be.

SCHING!

Askell appeared at the end of my sword and screamed. The strap of his Cloak of Mirrors split in two where my sword had struck his shoulder. The mirrors clattered to the ground. Askell brought a hand to his neck and pulled it away, red with blood. Once again I saw that same frightened expression on his face I'd seen in the depths of the Sunken Castle. A mix of astonishment and fear.

I smirked. "I see you, Semueld."

Askell snarled and raised his sword. The rust on its blade shone in the morning sun like drops of acid.

I parried his blow. And this time, I didn't step back. Instead, I responded with a half-lunge. Now it was Askell's turn to parry.

Then he retreated.

He's on the defensive, I realized. *He's balancing his steps and waiting to counterattack. Don't let him.*

It's not a dance, a voice in my head said.

It's not a game, another said.

It's a hunt, a third voice stated. *And you're not the prey.*

It was great having all those voices cheering me on.

While Askell and I were having our sword fight, Professor Everett tried to escape. He ran around the fire, trying to get to his van. Instead, he found himself facedown in the dirt.

"Where do you think you're going?" I heard my mother say. I stole a glance to see she'd tripped Everett.

The professor got back to his feet with the quickness of a petty thief and the same cowardly expression.

"Let me go!" Everett yelled. "You can't make me do anything! Stay back! I have your son inside here!"

And he pointed to the book from crazy Abdul's library. He pulled what he thought was the copy of *The Old Curiosity Shop* out of the paper bag and held it close to the fire. "Take another step toward me . . . and I will burn him alive!"

My mother leveled her rifle at him. "Don't you dare, Everett," she said with steely resolve.

"Don't challenge me, woman!" he screeched.

Using the copy of *Through the Looking Glass* as a shield, he took another step back toward the van.

"Yes, that's right, just let me go," Professor Everett babbled. "Don't you dare move a muscle and nothing will happen to your precious Doug . . ."

A smirk appeared on my mother's face. Doug was waving at her from behind the van.

My mom lowered the rifle just enough for the professor to lower the book. Everett backed up faster and stumbled, losing his grip on the book. It fell to the ground and opened, but he dove on it and picked it back up, quick as a cat.

"Don't move!" he ordered my mom once more.

He raised the book, turned it in his hands, and accidentally looked inside. He let out an unearthly cry of despair as his body turned to ink. A moment later, he disappeared into the pages of *Through the Looking Glass*. The book closed in midair like a bear trap and fell to the ground, rolling into the blaze.

The cover caught fire. The air stank of burned skin. My mother ran over and kicked it away from the flames.

Doug stomped on the cover until the fire was out. "Nice work, Mom!" he said.

Only then did my mother completely lower her rifle. "Doug!" she yelled. "Help your brother!"

Taking advantage of my distraction, Askell managed to graze my right leg with his sword. It sliced through my jeans and left a jagged, crimson line in my thigh. It was one of those wounds that — if I survived — would become a pretty cool scar to show girls.

217

It hurt like hell, but I didn't scream. Instead, I channeled all my pain into a mighty swing of my sword, which sent Askell reeling to the side. I did a half-spin, putting us face to face once again.

Semueld Askell's wound had stained his clothes in an increasing pool of violet. Yet a smile crawled across his face.

Behind him, my father, Reverend Prospero, and McBlack stared at us in awe. Somehow they knew, as I did, that this fight was mine — and mine alone.

And I was exhausted. I'd been distracted, and Askell had finally gotten through my guard. That meant I was running out of energy.

"I believe we've come to the end of the game, McPhee," Askell said. I saw his eyes track behind me.

That's when I realized I'd backed up to the edge of the cliff with the sea behind me. I was cornered and there was no escape.

That was why Askell had smiled. He wasted no time and attacked me with a series of quick slashes, the only purpose of which was to back me up and tire me out.

Lightning Launcher deflected the blows, but now its movements were a fraction of a second slower than before. Askell's rusty sword split open my jeans again. A frighteningly quick thrust nicked my ribs. I screamed.

I was cornered and had to get my back away from the cliff at any cost. After the next attack, I dove forward with a ridiculous somersault that made my head smash against the pebbles. Fortunately my awkward dive surprised Askell enough that I was able to get past him.

Rising to my feet, I raised my sword and parried his blow while regaining my balance. A moment later, I found myself on the ground without knowing how I got there. I saw Askell's blade coming down on my head and turned to my side just in time for the blade to slash into the pebbles next to my ear. I rolled to my knees only to find Askell grinning down at me with his sword pressing against my neck.

Game over, I thought.

"I wouldn't do that if I were you," came a deep voice from behind us.

It seemed as if the fire itself was speaking, but I knew instantly it was Locan Lily, Aiby's father. Slowly he advanced toward us.

I took advantage of Askell's confusion to roll away and jump back to my feet. I clutched the hilt of my sword shakily, hoping Locan had more in store for Askell than a moment's distraction.

I saw that Mr. Lily wasn't alone. Aiby was with him, too. So were Meb and Mr. Yuram Legba. The three Van de Maya sisters were there as well, along with Alejandro and Maria Tiago. Teobaldo Scarselli and the two young Moogleys stood behind them. And each and every one of them was furious.

McBlack had never stopped aiming at Askell — neither had my mom. My brother had Professor Everett's list of books in his hand, and he was reading the books aloud.

Askell backed toward the cliff. He slowly lowered his sword and forced a ghost of a smile. "All against one, eh?" he said. "Is this the Lily family's idea of honor?"

"You're a disgrace to your family, Semueld!" Yuram Legba snarled. "You are in no position to talk about honor."

"Throw down your sword," Locan Lily commanded.

I was trembling so much I could barely keep my sword aloft. Tears made my vision hazy.

Askell dropped his sword on the ground.

"It'll return to his hand," I said, warning them.

"Surrender now, Askell," Teobaldo Scarselli said. He wore an elegant white linen suit. "It's over."

Askell laughed hoarsely, reminding me of a sick animal. Then he gripped what was left of his cloak and yanked it across his face.

Where Semueld Askell had been, four black crows appeared, then flew toward the cliff.

Locan Lily looked into the morning sky. He raised his right hand. With a heavy heart, he lowered it in one fell swoop.

The seagulls all rose into the air. White wings, beaks, and claws surrounded the crows.

Askell's end was quicker and more terrible than I ever could have imagined.

The shrieks of the birds suddenly disappeared. Everything grew silent and still.

I fell to my knees and planted my sword in the ground. Someone ran over to me. I felt her presence even before she placed her hands on my face.

They were cool on my burning skin.

"Finley!" Aiby exclaimed on that long Sunday morning. "Finley!" Pearls of tears beaded in her eyes, and that was something I hadn't expected.

I smiled at her, revealing a freshly chipped tooth. "It took you a while to finish that book, huh?" I teased. She giggled and hugged me tight.

I heard Patches racing toward me and finally let myself pass out in peace.

Chapter
TWENTY-FIVE

FAMILIES,
TOWNSFOLK, &
FRIENDS

Reverend Prospero loved to say that you should never waste anything in life, so we all decided to use the giant fire that was already lit for an evening barbecue.

It turned out to be a good idea. As Doug, Aiby, and her father gradually freed all the people of Applecross out of their bookish prisons, many of the townspeople decided to stick around, talk about the day's events, and have something to eat. Aiby brought out the leftover drinks from the Emporium's opening and set up a few tables and chairs so people could sit.

I stayed on the porch at the front door. The whole time Aiby set tables and talked and handed out food, my eyes never left her. It felt like I hadn't seen her in months.

Yeah. I'd missed her that much.

"Oh, I'm so sorry!" she said when she bumped into something with her long, heron-like arms. That is if herons had arms — well, you know what I mean. I'd forgotten she was so long and tall. Probably ten inches taller than me, but right then I didn't mind.

My mother handed me a cup of elderberry juice and smiled so warmly I thought I'd melt. "Thank you," was all she said.

I liked her better like this, wearing an apron and a warm smile instead of snarling with a rifle at her shoulder. Still, it was nice to know she was more than just the mom I'd grown up with. I felt kind of dumb for not having figured that out long ago.

My eg had been bandaged by Mr. Lily. Now it was stretched out in front of me on a footstool. All the other Emporium shopkeepers had come over to introduce themselves, and every one of them felt compelled to tell me how brave I'd been. I especially liked what Mr. Legba said, because it had a legendary quality to it. I won't say what he said because it'll sound like I'm bragging, but I can't say I disagreed with his statement.

At the Emporium's grand opening, I'd spoken with Alejandro Tiago about the advice he'd given to the Lilys. Now, he told me everything had gone as he'd predicted — better, even. He was glad the Lilys had taken his advice.

Aiby explained what he'd meant. "Alejandro is an expert at reading tarot cards," she said. "And he gave us some useful information about what might happen at the meeting. He hadn't gotten everything right, but it was enough so that we were prepared for what happened."

Have I ever mentioned Aiby's beautiful, radiantly green eyes? Even after I'd realized those eyes had pulled me into a world where I'd risked my life in a battle with Semueld Askell, they remained my favorite sight in the world. Perhaps even more so after the fact.

Anyway, Teobaldo Scarselli congratulated me with a touch of his fingers to his white Panama hat. The three Van de Maya sisters — April, May, and June — were every bit as beautiful as they were friendly. While they spoke with me, I saw Doug staring at them. That was when I finally figured out why Doug had insisted on going to the meeting of the families. Sure, he'd wanted to impress someone — but not Aiby like I'd assumed. After the sisters finished thanking me, he told me he hadn't said anything about them because he was afraid he'd get rejected. But no matter how hard I pushed him, he refused to tell me which sister he had eyes for. Knowing Doug, it might've been all three of them.

Then Doug gave me back the key with the scorpion on the handle — the defender's key — without ceremony or apology. "Here it is," he said, not the least bit embarrassed. "I told you three. And three it was."

He had said three days, but he had meant three sisters. Regardless, it felt good to hold the scorpion key in my hand once again.

"Hey, Doug," I said, smiling. "What is something that those who make it sell it, those who buy it don't use it, and those who use it fear it?"

Doug shrugged. "Who cares," he said. He ran over to Aiby and asked permission to use the Lilys' rowboat. From the way Doug smiled as he headed over to the sisters to invite one (or all) of them to join him for a sunset at sea, I knew it'd be a memorable Sunday evening for my big dumb brother no matter what happened.

The reverend and I sat together on the cool porch. He'd been showily bandaged where Askell's sword had hit him, and a whole series of amazing ointments had been applied. Mr. Lily assured him he'd recover fully. In the evening glow, he seemed a paler than he had earlier.

"How are you doing, Reverend?" I asked.

He clenched his teeth and said, "Don't think I've forgotten about your rocks. How far along are you?"

I gave him a thumbs-up.

McStay jumped out of a cursed edition of *The Diamond as Big as the Ritz* by F. Scott Fitzgerald only to find out that his inn was fully booked that evening. That was fine with him as long as someone quickly found his wife (who turned out to be hidden on page 114 of *Wuthering Heights*).

Angus went to get meat for the barbecue as soon as he leapt out of *Moby Dick*. Seamus the TV antenna installer — fresh from his long stay in *The Penultimate Truth* by Philip K. Dick — was entranced by the Emporium, having never before laid eyes on it.

"Which satellite do you have the dish pointed toward?" he asked Mr. Lily, but he never got an answer.

My father was in an excellent mood. He checked on my health at least twenty times, as if each time he intended to say something to me but never managed to. I wondered what he wanted to say, but didn't press him because I was preoccupied by greater mysteries . . .

I asked Meb why she had sent me the copy of *Through the Looking Glass*. Her answer also revealed how Prospero, McBlack, and my parents had avoided falling into their own book traps: it had all been Jules's fault. In his customary bungling, he'd delivered Prospero's book to Meb (in addition to the one meant for her) by mistake. She became suspicious and called the reverend to her shop. The two of them sat on her sofa and Meb opened the copy of *The Master and Margarita* and disappeared into its pages instantly. The reverend immediately took the book with him and threw *Through the Looking Glass* into Meb's suitcase (which was actually my Stay-at-Home Suitcase) and chased down Jules for an explanation.

The reverend then forced Jules to read Meb's book — which was how she escaped from it. Then the reverend had Jules read the book intended for the reverend, and Jules disappeared. At that point, the reverend sounded the alarm for everyone to not open their books, but by then it was too late.

After Meb finished explaining, I had one remaining question: who had read my parents out of their books without Everett knowing? Meb didn't know, and Prospero refused to speak on the subject. Nothing more was said about that — until two distant aunts of mine emerged from the pages of *Pride and Prejudice* several days later, perfectly content with their adventure in Jane Austen's fictional world. Apparently, getting lost inside a book could be a good thing — if the books were kept safe.

For the sake of completeness, I should mention that Mr. Lily had been trapped inside *Niels Klim's Underground Travels* by Ludvig Holberg, and Aiby had spent a few hours in *Siddhartha* by Hermann Hesse.

When Aiby returned, I asked her what it had been like inside her book.

"It was sort of stuffy," Aiby explained. "You can move, but not much. You can talk with the other characters, but they repeat the same lines over and over. And when I looked beyond the borders of the town, the horizon faded into a grayish nothingness."

"That sounds like a pretty good description of Applecross to me," I said. Aiby rolled her eyes.

The rest of the townsfolk started to head home, chatting excitedly to each other about Captain Nemo, Josephine March, and Wendy Darling as if the fictional characters were friends they'd recently made.

"My father said that the effects of the stories will fade from their memories after a couple of nights," Aiby said. "And then all of us will just think we read the books instead of having lived inside them."

I told Aiby all about my trip and the trials I had overcome, but I skipped the part about the figures I'd seen in the mirrors. I wasn't ready to talk about that yet.

Darkness soon fell. Even though Doug hadn't returned from his boat trip yet, my parents decided to head home anyway. It wasn't clear to me if I should stay overnight at the Enchanted Emporium, or if the Lilys would take me back home, but I didn't care.

Because, finally, only Aiby and I were left.

Chapter
TWENTY-SIX

EPILOGUE

When the breeze over the sea gave me the right inspiration, I said, "Listen, Aiby, I . . ."

She slipped her hand in mine and all my sweet words crumbled like sand beneath a wave.

"I know," she said. "And I'm still very sorry. None of us guessed that Askell would dare to go as far as he did."

I didn't want to tell her about Imagami and how much I'd heard when I was hidden behind the screen. Nor did I like the idea of talking about the reflections I'd seen in the mirrors. It wasn't the right time. Maybe it never would be.

"Have the families decided what to do?" I asked.

"We'll find someone to take the Askell family's place among the seven families," she said. "Maybe."

At night, Aiby's lips seemed to sparkle. I sighed. "Anyway, I wanted to tell you —"

She placed a finger on her lips. "I know," she said.

"— about Angelica," I finished.

Yeah, I panicked. Sue me.

Aiby tilted her head. "What about Angelica?"

My face turned red. "I think I left her in the boat, on Skyle Island," I muttered. "And, um, I may have bitten her . . . and Patches buried her twice."

Aiby laughed. "Finley, Finley," she said. "It doesn't matter. You were terrific." Her eyes shone in the moonlight. "You've done more for me than anyone else ever has."

I felt like a teddy bear in a clothes dryer.

The space between us was smaller than a box of cookies, yet it also seemed as infinite as the entire universe. Philosophers probably have some fancy name for that sensation. We thirteen-year-olds just call it *panic*.

Aiby lowered her face a little but kept her eyes locked on mine. "But there is, however, one thing you still haven't done," she whispered, leaning in closer.

She wants me to kiss her she wants me to kiss her she wants me to kiss her! kept repeating in my head. But I decided to play it cool. "And that would be?" I whispered.

"I told you to burn the letter I had Doug deliver to you," she said.

"Oh, right, I said, flustered beyond belief. "Yes, about that . . . I forgot."

I leaned in closer. For the second time, our noses touched. Aiby closed her eyes . . .

And right at that moment, Mr. Lily walked out the door and ruined everything. "Did you turn on Mom's computer again?" he asked. Then he saw us inches apart and his eyes went wide. "Oh, sorry. I didn't realize . . ." Mr. Lily trailed off, turned, and went back inside.

Aiby and I burst out laughing.

"I'm so sorry about my dad," Aiby whispered.

"It's no big deal," I whispered back.

Aiby rolled a little snow globe back and forth in her hands. I knew it had to be a magical object, but I wasn't sure what purpose it served.

"Will you tell me what that thing does?" I asked.

"Certainly," she said. "But not before I thank you the way I should, Finley McPhee."

And she kissed me.

Oh, how she kissed me. Aiby Lily didn't just brush her lips against mine and pull away. No, she kissed me deeply with her eyes closed. At least I think her eyes were closed, because mine were. Then she placed her hands around my back and hugged me.

So I hugged her too, squeezing her tightly.

It was perfect.

When Aiby's lips finally left mine, I kept my eyes closed for a moment longer. I heard the snow globe turn in Aiby's hands, so I opened my eyes. The snow inside the globe began to fall softly on the small town below. Aiby giggled.

A moment later, I found myself back at the farm.

I was breathless. *Dang it,* I thought. I didn't even get to ask if the seven voices in my head were real or not. Or how long the other families would stay in Applecross. Or what we should do now, if there was something to do at all.

I didn't even get to ask . . . well, tons of other things. I shrugged. *What's the rush?* I thought. I closed my eyes and relived that last moment with Aiby, then went inside. I went up to my room. No one else was home yet, so I lit the little pieces of Aiby's letter with a lighter as I'd promised I would. As they burned, spirals of smoke swirled out the window, up into the sky, and dispersed among the stars. Then, suddenly, the stars that dotted the sky began to form lines, as if someone was connecting the dots between them.

It looked like writing. I rubbed my eyes, but the words remained. I read a sentence that made me blush from the tip of my toes to the top of my head. Aiby had written me a love note in the stars.

"Jeez," I murmured. "If I'd read this note first, I would've avoided lots of worrying."

I sat there, staring out my window at the celestial note left just for me.

I sighed contentedly. Just then, I felt a heavy hand rest upon my shoulder. I turned to see my father looking down at me.

"I don't think I'll bother to ask how you managed to beat us home, Finley," he said. "But there is one thing I want to tell you, son."

My father looked at me a long time, squeezing my shoulder so hard it almost hurt. "You can keep the thirty bucks you borrowed from me," he said finally.

He left my room without another word. That's how it works between men like us: the important stuff is understood, not spoken. *I love you too, Dad*, I thought.

My mom, however, lingered in my room a little longer. "We're very proud of you, Finley," she said. I didn't look at her. "We're afraid, proud, and happy — all at the same time. When I was there today, I saw my two sons just as I'd always hoped they'd be."

We hugged each other. I kept my eyes on the stars in the sky until we pulled apart. "Did you see them too?" I asked, pointing at the words written in the stars.

My mom glanced at the sky. "Of course," she said. "They're priceless, don't you think?" Then she ruffled my hair and left my room.

She can't read the words, I realized. *They're just for me. All for me.*

I loved looking up at that huge, infinite sky and pondering the great mysteries of life. There was something magical in it, something that made sense only when wonder still remained. Something that couldn't be explained in the words of any language in the entire world — not even Incantevole.

And these words were mine, and mine alone . . . but no way would they stay trapped within the pages of a book.

ENCHANTED EMPORIUM

36 EGGSTONES HEAVEN   APPLECROSS, SCOTLAND

ℙIERDOMENICO ℬACCALARIO

I was born on March 6, 1974, in Acqui Terme, a small and beautiful town of Piedmont, Italy. I grew up with my three dogs, my black bicycle, and Andrea, a special girl who lived five miles uphill from my house.

During my boring high school classes, I often pretended to take notes while I actually wrote stories. Around that time, I also met a group of friends who were fans of role-playing games. Together, we invented and explored dozens of fantastic worlds. I was always a curious but quiet explorer.

While attending law school, I won an award for my novel, *The Road Warrior*. It was one of the most beautiful days of my entire life. From that moment on, I wrote and published my novels. After graduating, I worked in museums and regaled visitors with interesting stories about all the dusty, old objects housed within.

Soon after, I started traveling. I visited Celle Ligure, Pisa, Rome, Verona, London, and many other places. I've always loved seeing new places and discovering new cultures, even if I always end up back where I started.

There is one particular place that I love to visit: in the Susa Valley, there's a tree you can climb that will let you see the most magnificent landscape on the entire planet. If you don't mind long walks, I will gladly tell you how to get there . . . as long as you promise to keep it a secret.

Pierdomenico Baccalario

IACOPO BRUNO

I once had a very special friend who had everything he could possibly want. You see, ever since we were kids, he owned a magical pencil with two perfectly sharp ends. Whenever my friend wanted something, he drew it — and it came to life!

Once, he drew a spaceship — and we boarded it and went on a nice little tour around the galaxy.

Another time, he drew a sparkling red plane that was very similar to the Red Baron's, only a little smaller. He piloted us inside a giant volcano that had erupted only an hour earlier.

Whenever my friend was tired, he drew a big bed. We dreamed through the night until the morning light shone through the drawn shades.

This great friend of mine eventually moved to China . . . but he left his magic pencil with me!